LOUISE

BY

R. LEWIS HEATH

R. Lewis Heath

ALL THE BEST!

◆ FriesenPress

Suite 300 - 990 Fort St
Victoria, BC, V8V 3K2
Canada

www.friesenpress.com

Copyright © 2021 by Richard Lewis Heath
First Edition — 2021

ISBN
978-1-5255-9581-3 (Hardcover)
978-1-5255-9580-6 (Paperback)
978-1-5255-9582-0 (eBook)

1. FICTION, AFRICAN CANADIAN

Distributed to the trade by The Ingram Book Company

LOUISE

1

The bees came.

Like a breakaway cloud, immense, growing, pulsing, burning – millions of conscious, armed and winged missiles, mashed together, spiraling downward through ice and fire. They came with singular intent; their roar shattering eardrums and shaking the earth. Buzzing and swarming. Stinging and stinging, transforming the very air with their ferocity. And they unleashed the deluge. Rivers of crimson liquid boiled and churned and flooded the world.

Then there was nothing. No buildings, no cars, no people, no air. Nothing! Except that gigantic, banshee-screaming funnel-cloud sweeping around in circles and engulfing everything! Beneath the whirl and the noise, she heard something else. A whisper? The wind? There was no wind. And she knew there could be nothing to carry even the tiniest plea from her lips.

Slumping to her knees, she felt the bees begin to drill their tunnels into her skull, her arms, and her legs. She was aware of them, boring mercilessly into the orifices of her body, enlarging even the pores of her skin, blowing her up like a giant balloon doll. She looked down from somewhere and saw the dark brown mass of them, moving, shifting, *flitting, buzzing, bringing her down, and turning what had once been her body into a husk. Like blood, they streamed through her veins, transforming them into a multitude of tunneled highways. She watched them, removed, as they moved hideously fast through the melting mound that she was and encircled her heart. Stinging and burning. Buzzing and buzzing. She burned until no breath was left, until she knew herself as only the flattened hardening remains of a wax candle.*

Then it changed. As quickly as they had come, the bees were gone. The buzzing was gone. The fires were quenched and replaced with air that was clean and fresh, and in front of her stretched a plain of endless darkness. There was serenity in that soft and silent cocoon and it claimed her, calmed her. She knew that she was not where she was supposed to be. But what did it matter?

In her living room, her car, her toilet, outside in the backyard; it was all the same. They were she, herself. They were the light and the dark, the awe and the wonder. They were simply dreams. That is all. Dreams that on more than one occasion had transported her into worlds that could be unimaginably violent or supernaturally beautiful! The subtle foresights she received from the dreams had often proved far more relevant than much else in her physical world. The long years and her father had taught her how to ground herself. The dreams, however, did not respond to any kind of opposition. They were often as powerful as anything she had known or could imagine. They came when they wanted and left when they wanted. She needed only to wait.

She waited as the darkness slowly began to recede, to fold up like a stage curtain and open onto a brightly lit auditorium. The room was vast, and many people were there; all sitting in cushioned seats behind the names of the countries they represented. She did not question her presence in the huge amphitheater. There was a familiarity about it. Deja vu, maybe. Or, it was a room she had seen on television a dozen times.

She heard her own startled gasp when the image sharpened and panned on the lone figure of a slender woman dressed in a gray pants suit. Surrounded by other people and standing tall behind the sign of a country that was blurred by the light, the woman seemed to be speaking in an animated fashion. Though the sign was unreadable, the woman's facial features were sharply contrasted with the rest of the room. Widely spaced eyes complimented a smoothly polished round face with a rich mocha complexion. She spoke on, but her eyes seemed to be intently focused on some distant sight.

Whenever she turned her head, her profile appeared as one that might have adorned a cameo locket. Her black hair was swept back into a neat bun, which sat atop the back of her neck. Her nose sloped gently downward, smooth and angular. Then, with shattering speed and no warning, the scene vanished, and the darkness returned. She woke.

Louise Angelica Throdmore Briggs listened to the quiet. The storm, the gales of rain and fire were gone. Only an unnatural, eerie silence remained. She tried to breathe, but there was no air. Then she heard the first thump. Again, silence. Thump. Seconds passed before she identified the sound she heard, and she knew that it was her heart.

Finally lifting her head from her folded arms, Louise gasped. Her hands frantically grasped at the edge of the table as the nauseous sensation of displacement swept through her body. It was sometimes such a wrenching experience, like a rupture in time and space where it seemed her very soul was being pulled apart. She inhaled deeply. This time air rushed into her lungs. She released it slowly, until the emptiness of her lungs was almost painful. Gradually settling into her regular breathing and feeling her eyes adjust to the light, she regained her balance.

Looking around the room in which she sat, Louise felt a giddy gladness cover her face. She loved the room's secure familiarity and she mentally hugged herself as the luxuriant warmth that she had worked so hard to create surrounded her and restored her. It was her kitchen, her table at which she sat, and the aromas that lingered in the air were from the roast she made for supper. Her faded yellow Amana fridge whirred noisily against the far wall.

The old brass clock she won at the Book Fair hung between the door and the stove and ticked in concert with the discordant music of the refrigerator. The clock was two minutes behind, but it was always two minutes behind. She had to fix that. She smiled as her eyes turned towards her blue African violets in the window above the sink. Though out of season, the leaves looked fresh and vibrant in the kitchen light. Sitting at the table with her and just to her left, nine-year-old Christine had abandoned the pad of foolscap and open geography book in front of her and stared woefully at her mother's face.

"It happened again, Mama," Christine said, her chin firmly cupped in her left hand and her young voice thick with accusation. "I know every time because your body gives this big jerk, kinda."

What could she say to her child? What had happened was no surprise to either of them. Reaching over, she took the girl's chin into her own hand and lifted her face so that she could see into the depth of Christine's eyes. Instantly, she experienced another sensation she loved, this one more intense than any other. She is a beautiful child, Louise thought. Her skin is much brighter than my own. No surprise there, she laughed silently, since her father is white. Wallace. So much of him is in her. Her face is like a heart, with lips that are perfectly shaped and which also dimple her cheeks when she smiles. Her eyes are large, hazel, expecting, usually laughing, and they peer out at the world from beneath sandy-brown eyebrows and a mane of thick and curly, reddish-blonde hair with natural auburn streaks here and there. This is my miracle, Louise thought.

"I'm fine, Sweetie." Shaking her head, she let her gaze fall to the pile of study materials in front of the girl. "Everything's fine. How's your homework coming?"

"Mama, you always ask that same question," Christine scolded. "And I always say 'fine'."

"Well, what do you want me to ask you, Chrissy?"

"No, Mama! Not ask. Tell!"

"Okay. What do you want me to tell you?"

"Tell me. . . ." Christine leaned back in her chair, lifted her arms over her head, and looked up at the ceiling. The imitation Tiffany lamp hung overhead and cast a colorful rainbow corona around the girl's head and arms. "Tell me if what happens to you is going to happen to me."

Oh, Lord, Louise thought. What is this? After all this time! Why now? She has witnessed so much, and she deserves an answer. What can I tell her? I know that people who suffer from mental illnesses of all sorts are encouraged not to have children. Heredity, and all that! It is a whole new can of worms. No one has told me that I am mentally ill. I don't feel crazy. I simply have these dreams. Can my girl inherit the dreams from me? Louise shook her head and yielded to the distinct and growing sense of urgency rising into her chest. I have run out of time. I must try to tell her the story as it was told to me, and I must do it now. She needs to know.

"Chrissy, you know how many doctors I've seen," she paused and watched as the girl stared at her with eyes that tore through the veil of memory. "You know how many medical examinations your mother has been put through. Well, there were others. Before you were born, other doctors and psychologists and psychiatrists were there too. When I was in university, I voluntarily became a lab rat hoping that I would find out what was happening and what to do to stop it from happening. It didn't take long before my brain felt like a pin cushion and there were still no answers. Nobody could find a thing. None of the usual brain diseases! Just the dreams! And they have never stopped. Though we never talked about it when we lived together, your grandfather now tells a different story. He says that what happens is because of our blood."

"Grandpa said that!" The girl's right hand reached to her head where she began to tug on strands of her hair. Her mouth formed into a small oval of surprise. "Does it happen to Grandpa too?" She squeezed her eyes shut. "And Uncle George, too?"

Louise nodded her head just as the tentacles of suspicion bloomed and spread through her thoughts. Something about what she was saying to her child was too easy. Something about the way Christine responded to her was unexpected and just a bit too comfortable. She had always thought that talking to her daughter about these things would be like jumping off a cliff into a never-ending fall. Instead, Christine's face registered nothing other than that of a child at play. Hide and seek. Yes, that was it, a game. Now you see me, now you don't. The girl was thrilled at what she was hearing.

"Cool!" Christine grinned broadly. "I love Grandpa. He's so cool."

"Did you talk with your grandfather about this stuff?"

The child shook her head emphatically. "No, Mama. He didn't. Well, not really. He just said that I would learn everything when I'm older."

Louise glanced at the wall clock. It read 8:30 pm. That means 8:32, in case anybody's interested, she chuckled. The small humor she found, however, did little to allay the feeling of being pulled in two emotional directions. On one hand, she could almost see her anger awaken and rise from some dreadful chasm and seep into her thoughts.

Why had he spoken with the child about things that were at best not clearly understood? It is too soon, she thought. She is too young. Then, on the other hand, she smiled as smidgens of gratitude toward him sprouted like spring planted seeds. He had made one of her oldest fears vanish into thin air. But then, as far back as she could remember, except for the time when he was not there, he had always put her fears to rest. She understood implicitly that her anger was laced with the deep guilt she had never actually understood, and which always seemed to exist between parents and children. As quickly and as loaded with personal implications, she saw her father. Her thoughts revolved around the old man, and she entertained some of her own feelings. She had not been the good daughter. She had placed him in that nursing home and that was equivalent to abandoning him.

She was alone with him now, and there was always room for reconciliation, a need for forgiveness. After all, wasn't it he who had abandoned both she and George all those years ago, left them in Philadelphia with their dead mother's mother and father? Sometimes she wondered if she had really forgiven him for that. She understood it, but that just wasn't the same. There was so much about him that was inexplicable, like the night when he found George. From that time onward, she just knew that he had radar in his head.

Though many years had passed, she remembered it all as if it was just yesterday. Shortly after midnight, when George still had not come home, he banged on her bedroom door until she groggily drove him to the rail yard. He left her sitting in her car in the parking lot and moved out into the black night. Whatever it was he had used to find her brother though had drained him and left him as nothing but a shell. She alone had witnessed as his heart weakened until he was finally bed-ridden. She had worried that he would die. He didn't. Just too stubborn, she laughingly toyed with him through the many months she watched his recovery. In the end, after finding no other way to cope with his illness, raising Christine, and working, the appeal of the nursing home as the inevitable solution became the proverbial light at the end of the tunnel.

She never knew exactly when George made his decision. Six weeks after that horrible night, he quit his job and one day she found him in the Furby Street apartment they all shared. He was hurriedly packing some of his clothes in cardboard boxes.

"I'll just put these down in storage until you or Pops can send them to me," he said softly. "Don't worry, Lou. It's for the best. We always know what we're dealing with down there. Remember? It's always been there. It'll probably always be there. I know it and I don't have to keep looking back over my shoulder because I already know what's there. If I stayed here it would that much harder to forget what happened. I'd be on the alert for the rest of my life against devious and deceptive people."

Then he was gone, along with a part of her heart. Within a month after he got to Grandpa Avery's house in Philadelphia, he had landed a job with Transit, met the young woman he would marry because they already had a baby of their own on the way. Now, he and Anita have three teenage boys and a twelve-year-old girl. Louise remembered how easily her sister-in-law became pregnant. After only four years of marriage, she had given birth to three of her children. Still, she could not help wondering about George. Did he fully recover from the assault which almost took his life? It was all such a long time ago. More than twenty years. Some things stay, she reasoned. Some things have a way of lingering long after they are come and gone.

These were the frightful things about the dreams, too. The shifts in consciousness, the almost visionary pictures she was left to think about, the prolonged inner arguments that followed at the end of each session were all potentially very dangerous. Additionally, every time they came, they left something behind: a residue, ashes from the fires of some kind of ritual of purification. Often what was left behind was nothing less than terrifying.

Today, it was the light touch. The photo album of her life lay open in front of her, displaying the faces she loved, blessing her. Yet the fresh memory of seeing the image of herself in another world tickled the very edge of her consciousness.

The internal wrestling matches dragged on for years before she'd finally accepted that the dreams were as much a part of who she was as was her father. She had, after all, inherited them from him, as had her reluctant brother. Perhaps it was outside the realms of reason to hope that Christine would be free of the dreams. The child was already a dreamer, and it was that fact that had cemented the relationship between Henry and his granddaughter. She turned the album's page.

In the early years, long before she was accustomed to being a mother who was forced to realize that this young spirit was not completely her own, she saw that whenever anything alarmed Christine she had run to her grandfather. Then, when she was five, unexpectedly and without provocation, the girl began to walk through the dream world.

Louise remembered that time because every member of her family went through the metamorphosis with her. For months, Christine endured long nights of spontaneous screaming fits, night terrors. She even became a sleepwalker for a time. She could only watch as her daughter behaved in a host of ways that were odd and certainly not expected of any five-year-old child. Everyone in the family made themselves available, but it was her own father's participation that was the most astonishing. When the child's fits reached a point long past her own capabilities and she was utterly bewildered, she had called him. Taking the bus from the old apartment where he still lived, he had pushed the doorbell at her house an hour later.

"I wish you had called on me before this," he said as he strode through the door and into the living room. "It's probably nothing more than memories from the past."

"I know I should have called, Daddy," she had blurted. "I didn't think it was going to be like this. Children go through all kinds of things. I thought it would last only a few days. It's been months! I'm worn out with this. I don't know what else to do. And you know what else? I am not sure who it is I am more scared for – myself or my child."

"That's simple," he replied. "This isn't about you. It's about my grandchild and what she's going through. . . . Wallace know about this?" Henry stood stone still in front of her. She felt his eyes boring deeply into her own.

"He's been staying here," she had replied. "He knows all about it, but there's nothing he can do."

"It'll be okay, Baby Girl," Henry sat down on the sofa. "What's for supper?"

"I'll put something together."

Shortly after he arrived, Christine emerged through her bedroom door and sidled warily into the living room. Her tiny face appeared pinched and tired. When she saw her grandfather, she ran across the room and jumped onto his lap. For the next few days the two of them were inseparable. Occasionally, Henry would hold his granddaughter in his arms and gently tap her forehead with the fingertips of his right hand. When he went back to the apartment on the weekend, Christine cried briefly. But her energy was changed, and she quickly began to smile again.

Louise felt her own energy change as she turned the album's page. Though memories of the dream, of the bees, were fading, she knew they would remain lodged somewhere in her consciousness.

2

"I imagine that some people think that when you get old, you're just supposed to either get sick and die or sit back and wait for death to come. And you better not wait too long. . . . It's like nothing else can even be expected of us." Henry Throdmore smiled wryly as he looked around the vast lounge room in which he sat.

This place reeks of lives lived long ago, he thought, of youth vanished, of disease and imminent death. He noticed that somewhere in the past the walls had been painted a bland pink and left unadorned except for a few cheap reproductions of Norman Rockwell paintings of rosy-cheeked children. Other people were also in the room, scattered about like pieces of flotsam. Two dark-haired young male orderlies, dressed in white shirts and white pants and looking more than a little self-satisfied, casually pushed occupied chairs around in a large circular space smack dab in the middle of the room.

Miss Mildred Whipple, the duty nurse, was there too. The woman never wears a nurse's uniform, Henry thought. Still, she's a mighty undeniable and formidable authority. More than once he had seen the young orderlies stand at rigid attention in her presence. Something else about Nurse Whipple perplexed him. Whenever the gray-haired woman's tall slender body passes you by, she leaves in her wake a puff of cool wind.

Henry laughed silently at the irony surrounding him. He wished for blindness as his vision filled up with the sight of the other emaciated bodies occupying wheel chairs throughout the room. Their bowed heads seemed eerily attached to the bottles of oxygen and IV poles standing by like indistinct relatives. An absent daughter. An almost forgotten son. Gods and Goddesses! In the left corner of the room, shiny gold wriggling paper streamers, left over from the Christmas party, dangled down from the ceiling. Over by the big window, away from the streamers and the oxygen bottles, the old upright piano is quiet and lonely-looking.

Henry wheeled his chair around to face his two companions, both of whom also sat firmly ensconced in wheelchairs. "And judging by where all of us are right now, that's exactly what we do. Just wait for it to come."

"Yeah! Well, I'd wager most of us would like for it to hurry up a bit too," Casey DeVries' large blue eyes sparkled an odd mixture of age and humor as he responded in that gravelly voice. "We got our tickets, but the bus is late."

"It's all about philosophy, I say," Raymond Levesque breathed heavily through the nose device he wore. His small oxygen bottle lay on his lap because Nurse Whipple determined that he was strong enough to turn the little knob at the neck of the bottle. Even recovering from a recent bout with pneumonia, the man is still a young eighty-four. He tells tales about the world he lived in. He taught at the university for forty years. That, of course, was enough time to become a real ladies' man! A man filled with new ideas. Any of his five wives would tell you that. Philosophy! That's what he taught. "A man needs a philosophy his whole life -- from the beginning to the end in this world. . . . I wish Victoria would play the piano again."

"Hell," Henry laughed. "I don't even know how she did it the first time. Them fingers are all curled up with arthritis. . . . I heard she was a nightclub singer back in the old days. I bet she was pretty good, too."

"Did she have a name?" Raymond quizzed. "I never heard it."

Henry heard Raymond's question, but it was only an echo. So far away! He offered no response. He could not. That thing from which he suffered had grabbed him again. His mouth was clamped shut and already he was adrift. He felt the dry hard fist of indigestion thrum against his chest as it had on several occasions before. Suddenly he saw himself flying through air, through space. Between and betwixt clouds, and up among the stars he flew. He knew that he was dead and that he was alive. The roar of his heartbeat ravaged his mind and hammered against his skull. With his eyes squeezed shut and gasping for breath, he clung tightly to the arms of the chair.

Nurse Mildred Whipple was there, like a cool windblown sheet fluttering in the air and gently wafting downward from heaven to cover his naked soul. He didn't really see her, but her scent filled his nostrils. Clean, fresh, sterile! One of the young dark-haired orderlies was with her. Henry felt the boy grab his arm. He felt the tiny prick of Nurse Whipple's needle as it pierced the flesh of his arm and he ceased struggling immediately.

"There, there, Henry." Nurse Whipple cooed. "Thought you'd take a little trip? Did you? Maybe you should just get some rest for now. We'll bring your supper to your room." She nodded to the orderly who instantly grabbed the back of his chair and wheeled it through the exit and along the long dark corridor that led to his room. In his room, the boy lifted him onto the high bed and raised the bar. Then he was gone.

"Not yet!"

It was a familiar voice and laying calmly on his back now, Henry opened his eyes and rested them on the poster-sized photograph on the wall by the door. One of the great surprises of his life was when Louise brought it from the apartment and mounted it with the nods and smiles of the staff here at the Home. It was him and Lena on their wedding day. How lovely she was. How happy they had been. How brief it all was. So long ago! He closed his eyes again and drifted off.

The vast curtain of light reached far across the night sky. Shifting light, shimmering colors, crackling energy; all of it was alive and held up by the stars. When he listened, he could hear its voice. Far beneath the curtain, shadowy darkness slid rapidly across a rolling landscape. No lights shone from the windows of houses for there were no houses. No path led from where he stood yet he stepped forward. His movement brought instant change to his immediate environment.

Suddenly, it was not night anymore. With the blink of an eye he stood in an open, sun-draped field. Summer heat burned into a parched land, but the trees and shrubs looked healthy and vibrantly alive. Other people were here, other creatures. He understood instinctively that logic could not apply in this place except to be illogical. The land was dry but there were pools of water everywhere.

A small curly haired child played at the edge of one of the pools and she captured his attention completely. The girl's entire being was wrapped in golden light as she held a doll in one hand and a tiny toy shovel in the other. Yet something was wrong with the picture of innocence he saw. He knew it. Then he was there beside the pool, beside the child, beside the source of his fear. He saw the spiny, poisonous serpent paused only a foot from the child's bare legs. He watched as with one gigantic leap, the creature sank its fangs into the girl's young flesh. A look of surprise masked her face, and she was gone.

Something jolted him. Was it the usual electricity traveling along his spine, tickling him, forcing him to open his eyes, forcing him to breathe and to acknowledge that he still lived? He couldn't be sure. He did know, however, that of all the trips he'd taken into the dream world, this one was perhaps more significant than any other. Its message seemed designed especially for him, too.

Suddenly, all the fatigue of his life was now just a horrible blend of fear, old age, bad health, despair, and an overwhelming desire for it all to be over. Moments passed before he understood that the laughter he heard circling around the small room was his own.

3

"One, two, three . . . and the music played." The song was almost a mantra in her head now. Each lilting, repeating word wrapped her in a cocoon of soft expectancy. Something was coming. She could feel it. She knew it, and she listened to the melodious sounds emitting from the overhead speakers with renewed hope.

Her father had suffered another stroke. He still lived, but only barely. Last week, Doctor Simons even went so far as to tell her to begin the preparations for his departure. This morning, however, Miss Whipple called, at her boss' behest, and said that there had been a surprising and significant improvement in Henry's mobility. His breathing and his heart rate were both normal again. She had listened intently to every word the nurse said and at the end of the call she laughed silently. "That old man will live forever."

Louise looked toward the bank of large windows in the south wall of the room in which she sat. For the moment, the place was quiet. Shortly though, the empty desks and chairs that populated the room would scrape noisily across the floor. All estrogen and testosterone! That's what it was. After more than twenty years in the classroom, she had seen it all. Some things don't change, she mused. The teenage faces and bodies of 10th grade English would soon be staring at her with youthful uncertainty and feigned indignation, questioning her. As always there would be some boisterous discussion about the football game. Some giggly talk about who was dating who. Nobody, she laughed softly, could deny the importance of peer pressure among teenagers, knowing that they are liked, knowing that they fit in.

Seeing their youthful vulnerability had always been what made her work less like a job and more of a mission. In her way, she became a missionary out to save the children, to provide them with what they would need just to survive in the world. She worried that in a few short years her own child would be there. So far, nothing about Christine suggested that things would be different. Not even the dreams, which she had noticed occurring far less frequent for her girl.

Now, as she sat at her desk and watched as the door opened and closed repeatedly and the students drifted into the room and moved with precision toward their assigned desks, she marveled at their diversity, their individual singularity, and she found comfort in knowing that she had already influenced each of their lives. Especially since she had finally managed to get them to relax enough to discuss more esoteric topics. These topics, of course, were intended to introduce them to real world people in a different way, outside the purview of normal Social Studies, and they were essential. Today they would begin their discussions revolving around religions, old religions.

Today they would begin to stand up with their papers in hand and they would read to their classmates what they had found through their research efforts.

She waited until the room was quiet again before she stood up and faced them. Her eyes immediately flicked toward the rear of the room. Some of the faces in front of her appeared eager, eyes gleaming with excitement. Others, who often chose to sit in the back of the room, appeared to be haggard and less prepared. She would have to wait for them.

"Okay," she said, "Let us get started on our new adventure. Let us see where it takes us? Right?"

She was especially pleased when the slender, light brown arm of young Nancy Rodrigues lifted into the air. Over time, she had become familiar with the girl and her parents. As usual, the child was energetic, prepared, and eager to display what she had found.

There was another thing about her work that, when she thought about it, made her feel particularly jubilant. She was sure it was a bi-product of the dreams, a unique gift in return for all the uncertainty. A kind of mental multitasking, she reasoned. Knowing, however, that most people would call her crazy if they knew, she was happy that it was only a few who carried her secret. While focusing her attention on the here and now and listening to the first of her twenty students begin her recitation, she adroitly moved to other mental worlds.

Louise nodded as the girl fixed her eyes expectantly upon her. Smiling, she watched as the child stood up from her desk. When she spoke, her young voice was smooth and enthusiastic.

Louise' thoughts, however, were once again with her father. She saw his face. She saw him laying uncomfortably in that small room he occupied at the Home. So little comfort came with knowing that there was nothing she could have done for him, even if she had been there.

"I have done some research on the early challenges of Christianity. Because some ancient Roman emperors saw themselves as gods," Nancy continued, "they were determined to eradicate all hints of any new gods on the horizon. Long before his arrival, many prophets spoke of the coming of a messiah. On hearing these predictions, the emperors angrily labeled such beliefs as mania, mental afflictions that could be cured in only one of two ways: the gladiatorial arena or the cross of crucifixion. Many people died."

Then there was Wallace, Louise mused, who seemed more and more driven to take them all on a trip to Africa. Or, somewhere! Why had she chosen to hook up with an anthropologist? The question, sometimes loaded with exasperation, was often in her head these days when she thought about her partner. After all, he was Christine's father and they all shared the same living space, when he was home and not traipsing off to some unknown part of the world. And she did love him.

". . . nothing could quite eradicate this new human faith," Nancy Rodrigues' voice rang out like bell as she continued reading her report. "If nothing else, human kind had found a religion that was free of the cruelty of sacrifice which was evident with many of the more primitive belief systems. Expressions of 'Love One Another' swept across the ancient and predominantly Roman world with a speed no one could have expected.

"Even in more contemporary times, however, Christianity has been challenged. Repeatedly. Though missionaries spread throughout the old world and the new world, many nations mistakenly dismissed the faith as arrogant because it seemed to ignore the fact that they had their own beliefs and preferred to keep them. There were many reasons Christianity initially failed to reach large masses of people."

Louise listened as the girl continued. While she was pleased that Nancy seemed to have spent a good bit of time reading and had picked up on some of the subtle nuances of human endeavors, she began to wonder what the other reports would be like. This was only the first of twenty and each would be accompanied by ensuing discussion. She was grateful that it was still only October.

Then, quite unexpectedly, Nancy concluded her recital, and Louise made her decision. She would gather Christine after school and she would make the trip to the Home. The drive west along Portage Avenue, beyond the Perimeter, and out onto the Prairies, she thought, could put her mind at ease. She imagined how miserable Henry must be and she saw herself leaning over him, fluffing his pillow, comforting him as if she were his nurse. She had to see him. The good daughter! She had to let him know that he was not alone.

4

Dr. Wallace Briggs concluded his last lecture session of the day with an open invitation to his anthropology students to see him in his office. He paused, removed the handkerchief from his pocket with one hand and took off his glasses with the other. He felt the soft cloth glide smoothly over the lenses then restored them to his face. Looking out over the auditorium, he felt uneasy. Though the vast room emptied quickly, he sensed his own impatience growing. Yet he waited until the last student exited before pushing his notes into his briefcase. In the sudden silence, he heard the lock snap.

The walk along the hallway to his office was filled with the energetic odor of academia, of old paper and clattering keyboards. Whispering voices! Open doorways. The day had been a long one, much filled with one anxiety or another. The call from Louise earlier in the day had also left him on edge. She and his daughter were probably already making the long drive to the nursing home where Henry clung to the final days of his life.

Wallace was tired, and he wanted to go home, but thinking about the old man brought a wry smile to his lips. The kind of anthropology he studied and taught included all the Henrys and Henriettas of the world. Against all odds, they were ones who survived, even when they were not supposed to. Often the social scientist in him offered little choice except to regard them as specimens. Things to be studied. Social examples!

With a degree of statistical precision, he examined the origins of his samples, the life paths they followed, and the worlds they lived in, which had once seemed so different and distant from his own Anglo-Saxon world. Then, quite unexpectedly, his own world had also changed. When his father died several years before he met Louise, and suddenly it was only he who was there to look after Lydia, his mother. There were no siblings, which he regretted. So often, he had felt inept in his efforts to try and comfort her during her period of extended bereavement. Little did he know that was only the beginning of the cycle that left him overwhelmed and unsure and often jittery.

His world view was no longer seen from only a white perspective. He now had a black wife who had brought unbelievable and calming changes into his life. And, he had fathered a mixed-race child, whom he loved probably a bit more than his own soul. And yes, he often thought, the differing worlds do exist, but they are always the same. Each is unique and loaded with a million unanswered questions. After spending numerous long nights talking with Louise's father, he had acquired, among other things, a new set of insights into some of the other methods people used to survive.

The old man had surprised him. In the beginning, shortly after he and Louise had decided to live together, the three of them sat in the living room of the old apartment on Furby Street. That evening, Henry was in a happy mood. With a series of jokes he had picked up from other friends, he kept them entertained with intelligent conversation and lots of laughter. During the meal of veal and potatoes he had prepared and the bottle of Beaujolais they drank, the discussion eventually turned to the topic that was uppermost in his own mind: interracial relationships.

At first, he was sure that Henry was going to tell him to get lost and leave his daughter alone. Instead, the old man had stunned him with a remarkable ability to see the invisible with astonishing historical clarity. He immediately turned to the history of race relations in North America, citing some of the old civil rights leaders in the United States and how many of them had it all so right.

"People have often told me that I would do well in a gabfest," he laughed. "Yet, all my life, I have lived with the fear that right around the next corner I will meet my fate, and that will be the end. So, you two will be living together. I am pleased that one of my children has decided to follow her own feelings. Sweetheart, you are much like your mom. I am sure she is smiling right now. However, do me a favor and remember that our choices are sometimes accompanied by consequences. Not too long ago what you are doing would have severe consequences."

"I know, Daddy," Louise nodded. "The world is changing, even if it is slow."

"Anyway, slow though it may be, we have all had to witness and come to understand the truth about growing up and living in a world of absurdity where some of our fellow human beings continue to think it is prudent to judge people, good or bad, by the colors of their skins. Now I have come to believe that it is humanly impossible for this to be anything more than classic narcissistic egotism at its worst, and it has nothing to do with reality. Look to the UV rays if you want a glimpse of what is really in play. Those other less reasoned perceptions, however, have managed to gain themselves a very firm foothold since the end of the American Civil War. There could be only one result, of course, and it was the mass persecution and murder of thousands upon thousands of black people at the hands of hateful mobs and the less than honorable members of law enforcement. Even now, this continues. Relentlessly. And, on world-wide levels! I never quite figured out what was missing until one day when I was working in the bush.

"There's only one thing, I thought, that makes any sense. If that ancient construct called the Rule of Law is truly all powerful, then why hasn't it altered all those negative perceptions of itself? It does so little to alter traditional thinking when it comes to race, a topic which was built into the nation building systems at the beginning. Why has it not found a way for all people to see each other as people?"

"That's not its job!" Wallace laughed. "It is a man-made creation."

"And it has somehow morphed into something god-like?" Henry questioned.

"Yes."

"One of the biggest problems, as I see it, is that the groups which are chosen to create the laws are always comprised of those already holding money and power and status. They often seem to be relatively immune from the harshness of life that most of us experience. Too soon, what was a brilliant idea intended to unite and protect all of us devolved into little more than a corrupt system of protection for only those creators of myopic and unjust laws. It was always of little or no consequence when and if anybody else got hurt or murdered or robbed, so long as it wasn't any member of those groups.

"Remember," Henry continued, "it was members of those same groups of people who had managed to get their hands on the kinds of weapons that not only intimidated, but spawned psychological animus, a peculiar type of self-loathing branded into the psyche of those who were not as they were. They got hold of some unique weapons, too. Persuasive weapons, sophisticated and image-building weapons, anything that would make themselves look so desirable that everybody else should want to be like them.

"Early movies out of Hollywood were always ostensibly popular, and always carried social messages that exalted the favored group. D.W. Griffith's "Birth of a Nation" was undoubtedly the most egregious. His elevation of those night-riding vigilante supporters of law and order, who were already responsible for the terrorist murders of thousands of black Americans and who were participants in the genocidal decimation of the American Natives, was beyond the pale and intensified racial fears. All those law and order, six-gun toting cowboy films turned just about everything into a blurred and eternal struggle between the "good guys" and the "bad guys".

"To this day, the war between the white hats and the black hats pushes the rest of us into tight corners of fearful uncertainty and despair. Talk about mass hypnotism! The threat of utter annihilation simply was the icing on the cake."

"You sound like an angry man," Wallace had said.

"I know. I guess I am," Henry nodded. "Even old people get mad. The real problem for most of us is this feeling of being trapped, like an animal that ought to be free. It is not some external force that holds us encaged. I often think it's a combination of old age and fear."

"But, Daddy," Louise chimed into the discussion. "If we don't have the Rule of Law, we'll have anarchy. There's just got to be something that offers us guidance and a sense of order and safety in our lives."

"Anarchy! You think?" Henry seemed amused at Louise's response. "Maybe I am wrong, but my faith lies in the hope that most people will do the right thing. Do you remember Muhammad Ali's 'Rope a Dope'? Now, there's a whole school of thought that teaches that we're the dopes and we have been roped. Make no mistake about this. Pure law is one of our finest achievements. Now, though, there are as many laws as there are stars in the sky. Just about everything us humans do is either guided or restricted by one law or another.

Henry smiled at Louise' response. "In today's world, my daughter, the Rule of Law often seems to have morphed into a bird from a different species. Firmly imbedded in the American version of the Rule of Law are many of those irrational Jim Crow principles from the late 1800s and early 1900s. Like insatiable vultures, they just keep on gorging themselves on the long dead and mouldering flesh of hate. They remain very successful, too, particularly at keeping the races at odds while imposing their power-hungry, unreasonable restrictions on citizen participation in the political process.

"No one," Wallace said, "can deny the truth of that."

"Sometimes, the Rule of Law takes a holiday and when it does things happen with astonishing frequency." Henry said. 'It is hard to follow the chronology of all these events as they are just as horrible now when they occur as they were then. During the early part of the twentieth century, the life of anybody in America who wasn't white was in jeopardy. So many lives were snuffed out without a fight or even a whimper and with complete impunity.

"I don't know if you have come across this story before, Wallace, but I remember very clearly that shortly after of my arrival in this world, people around me were suddenly speaking only in whispers. I must have been four or five years old then. Later, I came to understand that there was another small black child in one of those neighboring southern states who was electrocuted by that state on the white fabrication that he had killed two white girls. Knowing that he had not hurt anybody, the only thing the boy could say in response to these allegations was: "Why do they want to kill me?"

Since not a single member of his family was invited to witness this atrocity, the boy was surrounded by nothing but malevolent white faces, the vision of which he would take to his grave. He was utterly alone when he died. Sadly, this also continues even now. Black youth are frequently being murdered with impunity, and you just know that the cruel hand of some unjust God is in control."

"I do remember reading about that incident," Wallace said. "And I agree with you. It truly does look like the lives of black youth, particularly males, is always on the razor's edge."

"So, it is not just my overactive imagination?" Henry asked.

"No. I don't think so. This too is the sort of thing that has been built into the system."

"Then I have to ask a favor of both you and future generations. Please be more scrutinous. Please do some serious investigations before permitting dimwitted, inept, unethical, and unscrupulous people to continue dreaming up oppressive laws to keep the already oppressed more tightly controlled? A civil war has already been fought over this question, and there is still no resolution."

"I truly hope," Wallace inserted, "that that is the very last resort for resolving social problems like this. I can't believe that this is beyond our reach."

"You may be right," Henry said. "I hope so. I am finding that the older I get the more unusable discoveries I make. There are, however, some things which are as certain as the day is long. For instance, if you give a fool a gun, even if he wears a badge, he will kill either you or himself. Be watchful. When and wherever one of these badge-wearing, violent representatives of law enforcement magically becomes a gang of badge-wearing, violent representatives of law enforcement and issues the command that you do as you are told, you must know in your heart that the word freedom is meaningless and that you are living your life under a Fascist regime."

Wallace remembered the pause that followed Henry's statements. He had tried to listen his own thoughts as the quiet slowly hardened into silence. He suddenly realized that everyone at the table, including himself, were staring down at crumpled napkins on empty plates.

"Does anybody else want some more wine?" Not waiting for a reply, Henry rose from his seat at the table and walked into the kitchen.

"Yes," Wallace said as Henry returned to the table with another bottle of Beaujolais. "I'll have one last glass before we to go."

"Louise," Henry called, "Please have a bit more wine."

"Okay, Daddy," she smiled. "But no more!"

After refilling their glasses, Henry reclaimed his seat at the table.

"I am glad you decided to stay a little longer," Henry said. "There is so much more to talk about."

"Daddy," For one brief moment, a look of concern covered Louise's face. "Are you all right?"

"Of course, Sweetheart, I'm just happy you came to see me."

"I can see very clearly," Wallace said, "a fair amount of distress for those people who refuse to think about these issues. It is and has been a long time since we have looked at those people who crave the power afforded them under the Rule of Law. My job often reveals a psychic disconnect and unhealthiness in the very souls of such people, and it seems to follow them everywhere. They live continuously with those things that go bump in the night. Too many have built the very foundations of their lives on racial fears."

"Some of my friends are members of the First Nations community here in Canada," Henry said. "Like them, the old guys down south also understood how that kind of spiritual sickness taints the souls of both the individual and an entire nation. Negativisms, like racism, has been around for a long time and it has become normal in society. In the end, all of this seems incredibly disheartening. However, if I said nothing about it, I would dishonor the memory of Louise's mother."

"For both George and me, there is no memory of her," Louise said. "There has always been much discussion about her, but like most children who lose parents early in life, and who do not understand death, we felt abandoned."

"Yes," Henry nodded. "Both of you were too young when she left us. As a matter of fact, your brother was not even born when she passed. The doctors immediately performed a cesarean section and pulled the tiny body from her corpse. I guess I went around a lot of corners in those days."

"From the things Grammie used to tell me about her," Louise said, "I was led to think of her as a heroine in some great drama. In a way, I guess that's exactly what she was, and that drama continues. Doesn't it?"

"Tell me, Wallace," Henry asked. "Have you experienced much death in your life?"

"Yes," Wallace replied. "In both my travels and with my own father, who passed away a few years ago."

"When it happens," Henry said, "it is never easy. Especially when you know the people who pass. Yet, aside from the fact that none of us have come here to stay, that death is a natural part of our experience. Yet, I still wonder sometimes just how many of us die in the wars we create? How many souls pass on during the natural disasters that wrack our little corner of the world every now and then? Ever calculate the total numbers who die on the streets of our cities and towns at the hands of some disaffected and disconnected fellow citizen or by their own hands? And, still, the world population of human beings seems to continue to explode."

"Fortunately, we're easily reproduced," Wallace laughed, "along with all our frailties."

"In some ways," Henry sighed, "you are right. It doesn't matter. Does it? It's the same all over. No. . . . I guess it's just about high time that we all start looking for a complete spiritual and physical makeover. I have this feeling that if any of us are to move forward, we need to be able to see with more than just our eyes."

"Amen to that! Let me make sure that I understand you," Wallace, who was always conscious of the words he used, found himself speaking more freely than he had ever done with other people in similar situations. So much had happened during his early years. He remembered that it was he who had amassed a fortune in debt in pursuit of an education during his young adulthood. He also remembered that was he who had written and published important papers that, in his field, brought academic recognition. He had achieved his doctorate, tenure at a university, and a professorship of Cultural Anthropology. It was also he who had traveled to other places on the globe and had met similar minded people. Yet speaking with Henry, he had momentarily felt that he was a student again, that he had forgotten something he had learned ages ago. "You're saying that spirituality will save us?"

"Of course," the old man nodded his head. "Unfortunately, only a few people listen to old men anymore. Never the less, I believe the first step is to acknowledge our own humanity. With that comes the awareness that innocence itself is pure mythology. I might even go so far as to agree with those who say that the very idea of innocence truly is a crime against nature when even being born is a violent act. No one ever seems to think that a fetus can carry baggage. Few people ever look to or claim ownership of those lives lived before the one they currently live. Every now and then, however, we just love embarking on these flights of fantasy to the land of purity. Don't we? Deep down in my soul, I believe that we all come here to live, to experience, and to be soiled."

"Yes," Wallace nodded. "That sounds like some of the tribesmen I have met in New Zealand."

"Yes," Henry responded, "it is also in the old testament."

With all the other things going on, Wallace thought, it is strange that I never forgot that evening or any of the other evenings spent with Henry. He suspected that he had unwittingly adopted the old man as a kind of surrogate father. And, as time passed, he found their time together was even more helpful than he had initially thought. Henry became especially important after Christine was born.

He recalled that during many of his research trips, he found himself encountering numerous people whose views about life and living were akin to some of the views Henry had expressed. In some of the cultures he visited, he found laws built around spirituality. Laws that reached back into ancient history. Some that existed even before recorded time. Some were constructed solely to ease human suffering. And, yes, some were and are used to cause human misery. Universal laws and cosmic laws stretched across the breadth of human existence. Ancestor worship or laws completely in tune with the requirements of nature were prevalent in many other cultures. He understood the origins of the Rule of Law, the need to be free from kings and dictators. Only the law could offer both protection and solace. Yet, none of the places he visited or the people he had met with practiced the Rule of Law in the way it was done in North America. Additionally, he had yet to find a single instance of the Rule of Law mantra applied equally to everyone. Education happens in all kinds of ways, he heard himself sigh as he drew closer to his office door.

Opening the door, he tossed the briefcase onto his desk. Then he turned to pull several sticky notes, decorated with smiley faces and curlicues, from the milk-glass window imbedded in the door. A cursory glance at the multi-colored pieces of paper told him little except that some people were late with their assignments. One of the less disguised notes, however, was a piece of plain white paper folded into thirds and placed inside an office envelope. It was from Dr. Thomas Moreland Yates, the department head.

"Please see me before leaving," Yates wrote.

5

Nurse Mildred Whipple was on duty and waiting for them at the reception desk when Louise and Christine walked through the entrance and into the lobby of Grace Home for the Elderly. The woman's stern look and gray hair always caused Christine to draw just a little closer to her mother.

Nurse Whipple approached them.

"It has been a little while," the woman smiled.

"How is he?" Louise looked at the woman with the expectancy of a child. "Is he bad?"

"Quite the contrary," Nurse Whipple said. "He seems to be getting stronger. But I wouldn't get our hopes up too high. The doctor says for us to keep an eye on him 24/7. Anyway, your arrival will give him even more strength. Oh, don't worry if he goes to sleep on you. Listen for his snore."

Christine's legs picked up speed as she raced along the corridor toward her grandfather's room. When Louise reached the open doorway, she paused and watched as Christine stood beside Henry's bed, grinning with every muscle in her face and tightly holding her grandfather's hand.

"I ain't dead yet," he called across the room.

"You're just stubborn," Louise laughed as she moved into the room. She placed the bag containing the new pajamas and robe she'd bought for him on top of the chest of drawers and pulled the chair closer to the bed. Finally sitting down, she looked at him.

Henry lay comfortably on his back on the high bed. His hair was completely white now. There was no indication that he felt any pain. His eyes were bright and alert. Only the age lines on his face appeared stretched and tired. Christine hovered protectively beside him, holding on tightly to his hand. Henry turned his head and looked squarely into his daughter's eyes.

"I been watching television," he spoke softly, slowly. "These days, there seems to be a lot of stuff going on. None of it is any good. All around us the world-view is changing, and humanity is looking for a different way. The problem is that nobody seems to know just what *way* that is. Religion just isn't doing the trick anymore.

"I have recently witnessed politicians in my homeland, the good ole USA, a country that has long regarded itself a "Christian" nation, refute the teachings of Christ and reject the children. That's a bad sign. The current president is a good man. His enemies are many. I am sure they wittingly operate against the will of that majority of Americans who voted him into office."

"Daddy, the world changes. You know that. Besides, what are you doing causing yourself all this stress?"

"What year is this? 2014? Right? Who knew I would live this long? Who says old people gotta stop feeling?

Maybe it's just my imagination," he continued, raising his voice just loud enough for her to hear his anger, "something to encourage a leap of faith that somehow our resiliency will help us through this. Cooler heads will prevail, I tell myself. Accentuate the positive! . . . But I am old and cynical."

"It's not that bad, yet." Louise replied.

"How is your brother? I haven't heard from him in a while. Are my grandsons okay? That place hasn't changed very much. Has it? What a lie it all is! It used to be white sheets, a rope, and a tree limb. Now it's a badge and a gun." He paused then said, "Are you dreaming again?"

"Didn't George call you last week? . . . How did you know?"

"Don't have to answer that, my girl. You have the mantle now. Everything will unfold as it will, as it is supposed to. But I want you to be on the alert. Something terrible is going to happen."

"You, too?"

"See," he laughed, "that's why I don't have to answer you."

"Other worlds, Daddy," she said softly.

Henry did not respond. Instead, he had suddenly closed his eyes, and he was breathing deeply. He had gone to sleep.

"Grandpa," Christine's face quickly changed its appearance as she clearly did not understand what had just happened and Louise could hear nervously. "You want us to go so you can get some sleep?"

"I will soon, Sweetheart." His eyes popped open immediately. He smiled and said, "Just resting my eyes. I'm so glad to see you and your mom. And I wanted you to know about these things."

A few moments later, Louise stood up from her chair and stepped over to the high bed. He was asleep again. She touched his arm. Then she bent forward and kissed his forehead. She had wanted to stay with him longer. There was still so much to talk about. He was much stronger than she had thought he'd be. But the signs were still there. While his body was almost frail, his brain did not rest. She checked the pillow beneath his head and gently pulled the paper-thin brown blanket up over his chest.

"We gotta go, Chrissy," Louise whispered. She was resigned to reality. He would leave her before too long. She just knew it. "Come on, honey."

6

"I am about to step outside of academic protocol here," Dr. Thomas Yates, Dean of the Anthropology department looked at Wallace over the top of his glasses. "we have been friends and colleagues a long time. To put it simply, I need your help. I want to ask you to join myself and other professors in doing something unexpected," Yates' bare scalp gleamed in the light as he began to clear his desk and moved a small stack of papers back into his inbox. "I am afraid that I chose an inappropriate adjective when I said 'unexpected' Anyway, be that as it may."

The man sat behind his huge, ornately carved, highly polished 17th century mahogany desk in his equally well-appointed office. As the daylight outside began to wane, the stained-glass windows in the room were simply the pieces of art they were created to be. The windows were always magnificent even when no light shone through them. Old pictures and artifacts from other eras were artfully placed in key positions throughout the room. Darkly stained, waxed wooden beams crossed the wide width of the white ceiling and swept to the floor in graceful arches.

It was a beautiful room, and Wallace always felt just a little too comfortable in it. Long ago, he discovered that when he entered the room through the door he felt that he was returning home from one of his long trips. Each time he visited with Tom Yates, he looked around with a mixture of admiration and a slight bit of envy. He knew the chamber's history, and he knew that it was out of another time. As far back as the mid-1800s, Heddon Hall stood as one of the first buildings constructed when the university was founded. Much of the chambers character, like the classic moldings, were never damaged when the basement and the main floor were once ravaged by fire. The moldings held steady and continued to scream proudly to those who like architecture. Often Wallace was left with only his nervous laughter at his own wishful thinking. Today, however, was not going to be one of those days.

"I'm sorry," Wallace sat down in the cushiony leather chair in front of the desk and looked directly into the man's eyes. He'd known Yates more than ten years now. The man was older than he by about fifteen years, yet still looked fit. His face, a bit pudgy, often displayed his emotional state.

"I'll come right out and say it," Yates continued. "Some of the other members of our faculty and I are concerned about events happening closer to us. Though much of what I am talking about is political, we also recognize the many problems which reflect the failure of fundamental cultural values in certain communities. We'd like to know what cultural strengths allow for the survival of those people who are most often ignored. Would you consider joining us in doing a research project closer to home?"

"Tom, I am still not clear on what you are saying," Wallace replied.

"We are all aware of the academic documentaries you have made," Yates said. "Those films are more valuable than you imagine. In addition to and contrary to what many politicians would have you believe, there is a moral equivalency to everything that occurs in our world," Yates' voice fluctuated between anxious enthusiasm and a slow resigned dismay.

"Making a documentary is what you are asking me to do?"

"Not just one," Yates replied, "but many. Consider the possibilities. I have a feeling that conducting interviews with those who live below the poverty line will excite you beyond belief."

"Hmmm," Wallace could feel his line of thinking begin to shift.

"My friend, please put on your other academic hat and remember that for so long we here in the west have placed ourselves on this pedestal. Our word is the right word. Our way is the right way. Not just for us, but for everybody. Hah! Just imagine the fantastic stratagems the propaganda people forged to spread that image. Fortunately, in so much of the real world, the world that is lived in by people on whom very little attention is bestowed, we think it is reasonable to expect that there are unexplored belief systems, customs, and cultures. I know you are already aware of all this, so please forgive me if I come across too passionately. This is, however, where it all begins to get crazy. We think that this is where the breakdown of those cultural values begins."

"Yes," Wallace nodded. "In belief systems. I can see that."

"Belief systems!" Yates grinned, exposing a mouth full of shining white teeth. "You got it! I know you have some ideas about this. On one hand, it seems that we, as people, hold belief systems about all kinds of things. But, as some of the other folks have come to understand them, belief systems also enable people to, if nothing else, survive in the face of lifelong adversity. That is often the reason these systems exist."

"So true. It could be," Wallace said, "a stimulating and exciting investigation. However, I am also sensing certain dangers."

"That is the other hand, and we must always keep it in mind," Yates stated. "There is a problem with belief systems. They are not born of some humanistic revelation, and they are very often destructive. The old slavers, for instance, were quite pleased when their version of Christianity was handed to the slaves. They figured it made the chains just a little bit more palatable and taught the unfortunate creatures who their real god was, which created an even greater tragedy since many of those people were suddenly forced to abandon the god they knew. And this new god was either unable or uncaring enough to prevent the terrorist destruction of even those meeting places the slaves and freemen created.

"As a matter of fact, because of the slavers' deeply ingrained fear of retribution, there was a time when these places of worship were banned altogether. It's something to think about. It really does speak to the fear-based guilt of the true terrorists. It speaks to the lie that even their descendants live with. If I am right, many of those descendants have already passed their beliefs on to their offspring.

"To the best of your knowledge," Wallace asked,aHH "has there been any kind of substantive change."

"While not everybody is afflicted by negative belief systems, many people are quite pleased to live their lives as if they are one to two hundred years in the past. Though we are passed slavery as we now understand it to have been, The slave patrols, however, are still here and they continue to thrive. They are a part of our conscious-ness, and our conscience. I also think we can safely say that very ardent members of all hate groups continue to hold belief systems that are dangerous to all of us. And, of course, we can't forget that differing belief systems have brought about the slaughter of millions.

"There is some good news, however, and it is that underneath even belief systems, we have discovered a level of the human mind that is akin to a wide expanse of unexplored psychical territories. That same expanse seems to contain an endless amount of information and we have already learned much. Among other things, we have learned that the expanse itself is divided into strata. We believe that each of these layers may contain solutions to many of our social ills.

"In the end," Yates continued, "I like to believe that it is our job to provide solutions to a great many problems.

I'm just old fashioned that way. Ready for the pasture, I guess. Anyway, our colleagues and I believe that, based upon some of the stuff you've done, your recordings will once again bring academic attention to the demographics of the here and now. We want to look again at the current economic status, the survival rates, and the circumstances in which many deaths are occurring. Whatever effective folklore we can still learn from certain groups is highly valuable.

"There's one other thing I should tell you. After a profound look at disparate communities where the populations are static, not growing, like the black community in the US, some of us are beginning to believe that a slow, but certain genocide is being done on some races. And it has been occurring for many years.

"The way that this is done is very interesting, yet stunningly simple. To avoid even the possibility of a public outcry, you must do it slowly. Imperceptibly slow! While planting your poison in whichever community you choose, you paint your victims as unintelligent dangerous criminals. On this continent, now that we are all properly schooled and conditioned, who is going to cry foul when it is perceived that the dying victims, all of whom just happen to wear the same skin tones or close to it, and who are alleged to be gangsters and evil lawbreakers? The reason that this is particularly odious is because we see it happening in other parts of the world, and in the same manner. Are you still with me?"

"Yes." Wallace replied. "But, as you say, this type of study has been done before." His immediate feelings were a bit stunned by what he heard Yates say. It was all old ground. "Besides," he continued. "What could possibly drive this angle of study? Except for the genocide aspect, thousands of these studies already exist. Many are on a whole long list of communities around the country. And we have offered our findings to the leaders of various communities, along with recommendations. At most, we get a measured and dazed response from those people who could turn things around. At best, the only action taken is lip service. Talk, talk, talk!

"I suppose you have a site in mind?" Wallace asked. He paused just long enough to hear the unexpected calm seep into his own voice. It unsettled him. Based upon what he had heard Yates say so far, he was prepared to argue against this endeavor, but he could not. Nor could he comprehend the sudden shift in his own thinking about the idea. He just knew that whatever it was, it was palpable, very conscious, and deeply worrisome. For a moment, he swore that he had stepped away from himself and someone else occupied his body. He simply stood and watched as Yates' words moved through his body like waves of light. His own response was infantile. He wondered why. Then he silently prayed that whatever it was that had happened had never really happened and would never happen again. "And when do you want to begin?"

"I take it from your response that we agree? Good. There's a big task in front of us." Looking directly into Wallace's eyes, Yates' mouth curled into a joyful and unexpected grin.

"Yes," Yates continued, "you are right, on both counts. It is cyclical. We have looked at it all before. We have the stats. But even statistics do not always predict change in our world with a great deal of accuracy. Just to survive difficult circumstances, when very little or no real help is offered, as you know, people tend to adopt any of a variety of survival methods and perceptions, some of which might even involve violence and theft. I should say, though, and this is something I keep having to remind myself about: While many survival methods are adaptable, they are also instinctual, a part of our anatomy."

"Yes," Wallace said. "But what about how people see themselves in the world? Do they see themselves as victims, victors, or martyrs?"

"I think that just about everyone knows that even our perceptions are usually based upon what we see, and then think about what we see. All three of the categories you mention are applicable. We must not forget, incidentally, that what we are taught is the bedrock of it all. Perceptions are often born from traditional thinking, and they eventually become parts of culture. What we need to learn is: what part of the human genome it is that triggers perceptions to turn positive or negative? The good folks over in Social Psychology might have something to say about that. We know already that disparate groups of individuals will come together when they are facing a common danger. What is it right now? What perceptual methodology, during these tough times, are some of the poorer members of the 99% using to maintain existence?"

"In answering your earlier question about where we will do our research. It is early, and many of these questions cannot be answered. As for when, give me a bit of time to get things organized. I do know, however, that the job will demand you spend at least two months on site. Wherever it is! We just know it will be closer to home. Much depends on getting the right kind of help right now. If you agree to this, when it is time you can take along whatever assistants and equipment you need. During your absence, Ms. Nerba will sub your classes."

"I hope hazardous duty pay will be available, too. Just in case," Wallace laughed. "So, where is it? I can't discuss it with Louise until I know that, at least."

"By the way," Yates grinned. "How is she and that beautiful child of yours? I must admit that your family reflects what I have always believed that a family should be. Our own three children are grown and gone now. Nevertheless, Barbara and I are happy with their occasional visits. When you and Louise hooked up, I was exhilarated. You two were adventurous enough to shatter a few of those tired old boundaries. I know! For some reason, I just needed to say that. Next thing you'll hear is a number of people questioning my competency!"

"Thanks for what you have just said," Wallace smiled. "We are happy. When Christine arrived, the dye was cast. I could no longer be without them."

"Anyway," Yates continued. "I think Louise's interests in social justice issues and her experience in a diverse classroom setting will make her a valuable addition to the upcoming discussions. So, yes, I would appreciate it if you speak with her about it. Once we have all the details in place, I'll be kind of anxious to know what she thinks. Don't worry! If you agree to this, I'll provide you with plenty of time to do what you need to do." Yates bowed his head.

"I don't know if you heard," he continued after a brief pause, "but I am thinking of retiring before the fall term two years from now. Otherwise, I'll just be put out one way or the other. I'll still be retaining my position with the University's board of directors, however. In view of my plans, if you decide to join us, please understand that I'd like to see us advance toward the completion of this project before that time."

"Is this your parting legacy, Tom?" Wallace laughed. "I'm going home!" He was tired, and he felt his energy levels sink to a new low. Momentarily, he avoided looking at Yates' face. He was totally unsure about what had happened here in this beautiful room, or even what he had really agreed to. He had heard, however, the two words that caused him to feel both seriously unsteady and an almost grateful tinge of elation: "The words 'genocide' and 'retiring' echoed through his thoughts as he stood up from his chair.

"In a way I guess it is," Yates said. "I've wanted to get the lead out for years now. Doing this might just get me out of here with some credit. Yes. This is my swan song, so to speak!"

Stretching the muscles in his legs as he moved toward the door, Wallace began to listen to his own questions as they rose from the pit of his belly. At the door, he paused and looked back toward the desk. He was certain that Yates was playing him, taunting him. Did the man know that he coveted his office, maybe even his job? "It could be interesting," he said. "I'll be waiting to hear from you."

7

"Some teachers write that to understand Shiva is to understand all of existence," young Maru Tremblant stood in the aisle beside his desk and offered his report on ancient religions.

Louise thought that the 14-year-old boy sounded not only at ease with himself, but confident that he had done what he set out to do, and that alone made her feel good. There had been some problems in the child's life when he was younger. A couple schoolyard bullies targeted him as weak and vulnerable because he wore glasses. However, with each of their surprise attacks, according to witnesses, Maru simply removed his glasses and fought back. For a month, the boy was in the principal's office just about every day after punching one or more of his tormentors into senselessness. His popularity among his classmates quickly soared.

Maru's young body was well muscled and toned. A few, almost invisible, scars stretched across his brow. Both his cerebral focus and the intelligent order he often brought to his work had long ago placed him among her best students. Now, after two years, he also carried the newly acquired banner of being an athlete as though it were a badge of honor. She listened closely as the youth launched immediately into his topic.

"Though the faith often focuses on reincarnation, clean living, and compassion and contains a pantheon of gods and goddesses, the belief in Lord Shiva is the heart of Hinduism. To further illustrate what is meant by "pantheon", even the Himalayan fed "Great River of Life", the Ganges in northern India is worshipped as a Goddess. Additionally, the Hindu faith is very logical. To believe in reincarnation and then fail to express total compassion for all living beings is clearly illogical, along with an incomplete understanding of the faith. Among the Hindu, different species of animals are considered sacred and are protected as members of the human community.

"Through the ages, the faith has spawned thousands of ascetics, holy men and holy women, who through long periods of fasting and meditation have achieved spiritual insights few people outside of the faith ever attain."

Maru read on for a few more minutes. Then, quite suddenly, he paused and looked up at the ceiling. Finally, he looked toward Louise.

"I confess," the boy said, "I can provide only a very cursory view of what I have found. If I have discovered anything, it is that I cannot explain this topic in the fullness I believe it deserves in twenty minutes. I would need many days. So, here goes!"

Listening closely as Maru resumed reading his essay, Louise leaned back in her chair. She felt her focus slowly begin to turn inward and was slightly amazed that more than a month had passed since they began reading the reports. Maru was the eleventh student now to verbally display his findings. Soon, she thought, the holiday season would begin, they would go home.

She knew she had made tremendous strides in her efforts to stretch their imaginations, and to get them to look with greater discernment at things outside the routines of their daily lives. Already, the progressive work they had done put them in the same category as that of first-year university students. Still, she hoped to have the readings completed before vacation time arrived. The sound of Maru's voice reading his work only prompted an even greater anticipation of the final reports. She smiled.

"The vastness of India," Maru read, "contains a population of more than a billion people. It is also a nation that seems to have found a way to accommodate the tremendous diversity of religious beliefs. Alongside Hinduism, Buddhism, and Islam, Christianity and countless others thrive. This does not mean, however, that India has not experienced its strife. There has been plenty of it. Much of it was religious.

"One of India's greatest leaders, Mohandas Gandhi, was a Hindu. This small and brilliant man peacefully led his country to freedom from British rule. His spiritual worship, his willingness to stand up for human dignity in the face of long periods of time in various British jails made him a national hero. After being named the father of his country, it was his lot to spend much energy on trying to resolve the conflict between Hindu and Muslim. And, for a while, he brought peace."

Louise felt herself begin to drift, and she knew immediately what was coming. More time had passed than she
thought since that evening when she dreamed of the bees.
Though she had immediately believed the dream to hint at
some sort of personal transformation, she still sought anything in day-to-day life that might be connected to what
she had seen. She silently admitted that through the years
the dreams were only rarely precognitive. Regardless, she
had learned the hard lesson of not only paying attention
to the dreams but also to those internal physical feelings
preceding them.

Looking at the wall clock, she felt her anxiety rise. It
was the last class of the day, and she needed to get home.
She needed to lay down on her bed and close her eyes.
Fortunately, Maru was approaching the end of his essay,
and that gave her hope.

"In conclusion," Maru finally began his summation,
"this writer, though young and lacking in experience,
believes that religions ought to somehow do more than
simply sell God by the yard just to acquire a following.
After-life promises offer very little to those who must
endure the endless suffering that comes from either
poverty or living in an unjust world.

"As in Gandhi's case, an educated and trained lawyer,
his faith gave him the strength to undertake the arduous
tasks of bringing dignity and freedom to many millions of
his country's men and women and children. His influence
spread to every corner of the world, and other leaders following behind him have employed the same non-violent,
faith-infused methods in the name of freedom.

As Maru finished speaking and brought his paper forward, the last bell of the day rang out. Chairs and desks scraped noisily across the floor as the students prepared to exit the room.

"Okay, Class," Louise projected her voice across the room. "I am very pleased with our project, so far. We have nine reports remaining. Hopefully, we will have completed those before the holiday. Be ready, at a moment's notice. Bye, everybody!"

The room emptied quickly as each of the students rushed through the door. For a few moments, Louise sat quietly. The end of the day. Sighing, she began to tidy up her own desk. Then, pausing, she looked around the room to ensure nothing was left behind.

Finally, she stood up and walked across the room to the exit. At the door, she paused just long enough to turn off the lights.

Dressed in brilliant greens and blues and yellows and reds, the two tiny marionettes danced clumsily across the stage. Against the night sky, one of the dolls wore a gleaming tiara and a pulsating pink organza gown, while the other one wore a feathery pirate's hat and a pair of tight, electric-green leotards. Round and round, they danced, repeating the same two-step move over and over and back and forth. As they swirled, their unmoving black eyes in carved wooden faces spoke only of a yet to be lived infinity.

She saw them. She saw the carnival stage suddenly mushroom in size. She watched as the strings fell to the floor, and the wooden dancers molted and were suddenly living and breathing beings, tall and exquisitely graceful. She watched them flit back and forth across the stage. The crowd grew larger and larger. Voices were raised. People whistled and jeered and screamed invectives into the night. On the stage, beyond the crowd, the living dancers danced and danced, oblivious to everything except the dance.

8

"We're not spring chickens anymore," Wallace said. "I'm already nearing sixty, and to be honest I didn't think that when I reached this point in life, I'd be doing that many trips anymore. I know I've always spoken about us all going to the Serengeti, but that was just for a vacation."

"Sweetheart," Louise began to reply. Before she could fully do so, however, and for a very brief instance as she looked at him, she felt something that was akin to an electric shock. The two of them had lived together for more than a dozen years, and maybe it was their busy lives, their separate togetherness, but the man who sat at the other end of the sofa and on whose lap her feet rested was not the same man she married. Perhaps it was because he had spent so much time in the sun and the open air, crossing the wide plains of whatever country he was in to gain knowledge, but his blonde hair was streaked with gray. His blue-green eyes were aged and peered at the world from a face that was tough and weathered. Only the gentleness remained.

"You're preaching to the choir," she said. "Neither of us is all that eager to be traveling right now. Daddy could pass on any day. I just got to be here when that happens. Did I tell you about our trip to the Home?"

She watched him as he slowly shook his head. Then she dived into her account of their trip, focusing on Henry.

"He was physically weak, but in fine form otherwise. For someone as old as he is and having just suffered a stroke, the only thing I found was that his brain is overactive. He was deeply troubled about what's going on down south. Like so many other people, he has witnessed this type of savagery through much of his life, but the recent murders of all those young black men at the hands of law enforcement is particularly hurtful and is causing him a fair amount of stress. I think he needs to see George and the boys before he goes. He needs to know that, at least for now, they are still safe."

"So," Wallace queried, "what are you feeling about all of this?"

"Fear!" She looked toward the wide window on the east side of her living room and the tall leaf-bare trees beyond before she turned back to him. Her eyes were cast downward. Then she began to massage her hands. She spoke softly. "Yes. A deep and abiding and horrible fear has gripped my soul! But, then, that's what the monsters want me to feel. Isn't it?

"I think about what my own mother would do if she were alive. She was an activist, you know. She'd be out there marching with the rest of them, screaming for justice, while knowing all the time that justice will remain elusive, especially for black people in America. I think that in the end she would be willing to die all over again.

"So, you see, dear husband. Anything we do has to include Chrissy. We were late with her. Remember? I don't want to be apart from her right now. Not in any way. Her presence alone connects me to a past that did not happen the way I wish it had. Mama was not there. . . . I know. We play the cards we're dealt. Right? But since when does a child understand that? It's too hard for me to even imagine seeing our girl live a life of unremitting dread. I just cannot allow that to happen to Chrissy."

"Where is she, by the way?"

"Wally, it's Saturday! You slept in. I've already taken her to dance class this morning. One of us is going to have go and pick her up in another hour. There's fresh coffee in the kitchen."

"Do you ever think about the fact that she will still be a very young woman when you and I are retired? And, yes to your question about me remembering. I remember a lot of things. I recall most clearly what you put yourself through to bring her into this world. No regrets?"

"No!" She shook her head. Instantly, her thoughts returned to those final days of her pregnancy. Her biggest surprise had been that at thirty-eight she was about to have a baby. She had borne all the requirements, followed all the regimens. Wallace was with her at the Lamasz classes, and she was in and out of Dr. Little's office every week. None of that, however, had prepared her as fully as she wanted to be when her water broke, and she was rushed to the hospital to endure eight hours of labor. The other little surprise came when she learned that her body was not as strong as she had always believed it to be, and she had sunk into a very brief coma.

"Of course not!" she replied. "How could anyone be regretful when a child is born? I wanted a child, and I got lucky. Had I waited another year, she might not have arrived at all, and I would have missed an essential experience for me. Not all women need to answer the old biological clock the same way, but I needed to know what it is like to be a mother. I am kind of wondering, however, why we're talking like this. Is something happening that you're not telling me about?"

"Yates has proposed a new research trip. It's his dream project, though. Some of the other professors are involved." He breathed deeply and shrugged his shoulders. "He hasn't yet provided all the details, but he assures me that it will be here in North America. Maybe even Canada."

"Well." Looking at his eyes, she smiled. "That might not be so bad then. I'm sensing it's something you want to do. Right?"

"Maybe" he replied. "What he has laid out so far indicates that it could be a pretty heavy lift. He also said that when everything is ready, he is going to request your participation."

"Mine? I'm just a high school teacher. What could I possibly bring to the table?"

"I guess we're going to find out," Wallace grinned. "This is his baby. You know, it could be that where he wants to go with this is some place that no one has dared go before. At least, not around here! He's talking some seriously inflammatory stuff, and it is here within our world -- not some remote location. I've agreed with him, in principle. I think it is best, though, to reserve any final comment until we know more. Besides, nothing is going to happen before the summer next year."

"Good!" She laughed. "You had me going there for a moment. My students are finishing up a very important project now. Next week will bring the end of it, so I'm not sure I even want to think about any serious changes. In the meantime, though, we'd better start thinking about the upcoming holidays. Is Lydia coming?"

"Try keeping her away," Wallace chuckled, "and you might have a fight on your hands. I'll go pick up Chrissy."

Lifting her feet from his lap, she watched as he rose from the sofa and walked back into the bedroom to get dressed. Moments later, he returned. Leaning forward, he kissed her on the cheek. Then he turned and headed into the kitchen. Trailing behind him, she watched as he paused just long enough to fill his travel mug with coffee. Then he strode through the back door to his car which was parked in the yard. Through the kitchen window, she watched as he backed away into the lane.

√6

9

"Everything depends on gaining an understanding about the reason for our being here," Louise spoke firmly but slowly as she permitted her eyes to travel to each of the twenty young faces in front of her. "On this earth! Right now! We've always relied on religion to do that for us. To explain! To tell us somebody else's version of what we should believe. To explore this manner of communication between people, we need to briefly examine the idea of belief systems.

"Belief systems are so fundamental to our existence, Class, that it is necessary for us all to muster the energy and find what it is that we most deeply believe about ourselves. It just might be that we discover something truly magnificent, something that tells us that it is we who are the creators of everything in our individual lives, good or bad!"

Maybe Daddy is right, Louise thought, and she paused. On this last day of English class before the holiday, she knew that her own senses were heightened. She was also astonished at herself for forgetting something she knew to be important. Balance and good measure are essential, she thought. Still, seconds passed before she was able to move on. Looking around the room, she saw the looks of surprise on the faces of some of her students as they listened to her. Maybe, she thought, something *is* going to happen. Who knows what?

"These last couple of months and the readings of your wonderful essays," she continued, "have shown us all that there are other worlds, other people who think and believe and behave differently than we do. We have covered Atheism through Zealotry, Ba'hai through Buddhism. I am most pleased. We have some questions to answer, however. So, please take notes.

"The first question we must answer is: How do we deal with the differences we have seen? In a world that is on the brink of yet another massive and violent upheaval, ours is a multicultural society. Many people have come to Canada from places most of us have only thought about or read about. We have become a rainbow of different colors, different traditions, and different cultures. Can we really believe that such a place exists where so many people can effectively communicate in different languages? Perhaps one of the most important questions we ask of ourselves and the country we live in is: Are we true? Have we really grown enough to accept and handle all human differences well?"

She watched and laughed with them as each of them sent their hands flying up into the air. At that moment, she was inclined to allow the discussions to begin, but remembered just in time that there was still one last essay to be read.

"We'll talk about everything, guys," she said. "But remember, we have one more reading, and it is coming to us from our very own Lisa Similchuk."

The girl appeared almost magically beside her desk, and she stood tall, sleek, and wondrous in her youth. Long blonde hair loosely caressed her shoulders. Large blue eyes sparkled her own unique style of humor as she looked up from the paper in her hand, smiling. Lisa was fifth generation Ukrainian. She was born right here in the North End.

Louise recalled the evening she'd spent with Lisa's Ukrainian Dance troupe. She'd later described it to another teacher as one of the most exciting experiences of her life. In addition to thoroughly enjoying the dance, she remembered, she was blessed with the opportunity to meet with the young dancers.

"In the far north," Lisa began, "beyond the Ural Mountains and well onto the Siberian Steppes, there are tribes of people who hold spiritual beliefs that are more ancient than any of our current organized belief systems. Ancestor worship is fundamental to the processes of each day. But these beliefs are not confined to just one part of the world. In every nook and cranny on the planet that is populated by human beings, there were and are devotees and practitioners of what is believed to be the oldest religion known to humankind: Shamanism.

"It is almost easy to see how this religion gained and continues an everlasting hold on the human psyche. The belief in something, anything, that is thought to be higher than ourselves seems to have always been a human requisite. There has always been a god, or gods. Because each of us has had so little contact with the God we are taught to revere, God has successfully managed to remain invisible, unknowable. It is, therefore, strange that when good things happen, we sometimes thank God. When bad things happen, we always blame God. As it has for many thousands of years, Shamanism offers a way for the individual human to speak with God.

"Currently, and in the past, for those people who need to commune with God and are unable to, relief often comes in the form of a shaman. Shamans were and are priests, medicine men and women, witch doctors, brujos, conduits between God and humans. They are men and women who live their lives with a foot in two worlds: the spirit world and the physical world, and they are capable of consciously interacting between these worlds simultaneously. They are human beings who are devoted to healing and who often hold an understanding of earth-energy few people are likely to see or to experience. And they exist in every country on the earth."

Looking around her classroom, Louise was amazed at the rapt attention other students were giving to what Lisa was reading. Even she could feel the charm, the growing magnetism.

"Many people in Asia and in Europe," Lisa continued, "believe that Shamanism is not only the oldest religion, but possibly the largest religion. The faith long ago abandoned any claims to regionalism and very quickly became worldwide in what could only be described as almost transcendental. The often described and much maligned mystical elements of Shamanism traveled with us human beings out of the very source of our existence, which many highly esteemed archeologists believe to have been Olduvai Gorge, to any and every destination we were bound for.

"It is now understood that Shamanism has been a redeeming grace for some of the world's poorer nations where the people live continuously with lack. Like so many organized and recognized religions in our world today, Shamanism has long held its magic, its ritual. Certain people have always known how to play with energy and perform incredible feats that mesmerized large groups of other people. Jesus Christ did it. The ancient Druid priests were famous for magic and the roles they played in serving both the Gods and the people.

"As stated earlier, Shamanism exists on every continent on this earth. From Africa to Asia to Australia and in all the places in between, the tentacles of the supernatural are ever present. Wherever human beings come together, the enchanting inner images of other worlds and higher beings captures our imaginations and remains a powerful force in all our lives.

"In view of all of this, a lingering question stands in front of all of us. How does a shaman communicate with the spirit world? Or, vice versa! The answer to that question is found in many different texts. True shamans are said to know how to invoke the spirits through ritual, and then later receive responses from those spirits through dreams."

Louise heard her own startled gasp as a new pain sliced at the lining of her stomach. In that one shining moment, she was sharply aware that for the very first time in her life she was hearing a necessary truth. A comprehensible connection, the kind she had sought for as long as she could remember was being presented to her. The blend of feelings, of psychical sensations vibrated through her entire body. Who was the student? Who was the teacher? What did her father say? 'It will unfold as it will'.

"We all dream." Lisa continued. "We lay down on our beds at night and we close our eyes and we dream. But most of us dream of things that are not shamanic. Most of us dream of faces we've fallen in love with, of memories, and of a thousand unfulfilled desires. True shamans, however, control the dream state so much so that they can move from dream to dream while knowing completely the substance of each of them.

"Finally," Lisa reached her conclusion, "the face of Shamanism is the face of all humanity. We all seek miracles in our lives. We all want to believe in a more loving and just world. And this writer believes it would do all of us well if we took a closer look at Shamanism."

Louise was beside herself. She sucked air deeply into both her lungs and her belly as she watched Lisa approach her own desk with her paper in hand. Of the twenty essays she and her students had heard, each had brought their own glamour or compassion, This one, however, was like a ray of bright sunshine. Golden with the promise of finding a new path. Above all else, she thought, I must be careful. I must maintain my integrity, and whatever professionalism I still have.

At a level she had never expected, she understood the connection that Lisa's essay had delivered to her. Though she had waited for it forever, only a moment was necessary for her to feel it in her soul. Finally, she thought, I am an intelligent woman. Why didn't I see this before?

Now I begin to understand my own father, she surmised. How is it that we can live with people our whole lives and still not know them? She could not forget that she and her father had been apart for ten years. Shamanism! Is it possible that that's where he has always lived? That is how he has survived. That is how he has healed so many people, including his own granddaughter. He said that 'I have the mantle now'. Is this what it means? What must I do now?

"I knew you'd make it," Henry said.

"What? Daddy! Is that you?

"Who else? I have waited for you. Fancy this! Here we are, finally. You have had a few very interesting days. Do you understand now?

"I'm beginning to," she replied. "I should probably be more confused than I actually feel."

"Good. You've had a lot of practice. Your teacher is on the way. Do well. You have a big job in front of you. From now on, you'll find yourself with healing skills you didn't know you had. First, heal yourself. Then heal the people *around you. Wherever you find there is need, you must try to be there.*

"*I wish I could stay with you longer, but I have some other things going on. Watch out for my granddaughter! I have seen some danger in her path. . . . I will be leaving you soon, but I won't be far. Both your mother and I will remain close to you for as long as you need us.*"

10

Wearing the new red-striped pajamas and the blue robe Louise brought for him, Henry lay atop his bed and stared at the large photograph on the wall beside the door of his room. The evening light coming through his window steadily diminished, yet he could not close his eyes. He already knew every detail of the picture, every crease in the aged paper, every scratch on the glass that covered it. The poster-sized photograph had been with him since that September Sunday in 1963, since the day when he wed Lena. If I have ever questioned the longevity of love, he thought, I no longer need to.

On that day and in a flash of a second, he remembered, the world had changed. A thousand miles away from the church, from the music, from the happy hopes and laughter of their relatives, an event occurred that turned a young man into an old man. A young woman shook with fear and rage and a terrible resolve to fight back in whatever way she could.

The preacher who had stood before them and pronounced them man and wife delivered another message, a message of death, of children murdered in another church by the predatory terrorism that was so much a part of the

American fabric and to which they were all accustomed. What dream is this, he asked silently. Who else was there to see the infinite interconnectedness of those actions, and the reactions?

Anybody!

No, he thought. No one was there. Nothing was there. Except for the loss of hope in that one moment, and the excruciating vision of such limited space and time.

It is not the same as if she were physically with me. Even so, she is here. Since my childhood and with every breathing moment of my life, she has been there. We had our time, brief though it was. And it never ended. It simply changed. And look at what we did. To the best of his knowledge, long distance love was almost certainly a thing of the far past, if ever it had existed at all. Even their children never quite understood it.

The memory of his long path and how it had held many distractions settled around him like a long-trusted friend. I wonder, he thought, if they still say that "just before the end, we do the summing up and relive our lives". He had often reasoned that it was the aloneness of being that was perhaps the most difficult of all the challenging distractions he had dealt with. That early discovery of the impermanence of everything stood as a glittering beacon of strength in the life he had known. The changing seasons always made everything right. Somehow!

Suddenly, it was so easy to see himself as a boy. On smoke and fleet feet, he flew over the red clay of Georgia and across the rolling hills of southeastern Pennsylvania. It was always the smoking chimney of his house during those snow-ladened winter days that took him home. The wood stove was always hot, and the aroma of good food was always there. Closing his eyes, Henry felt himself begin to drift. He could move through time, through space, and know that he had lived it, know that he too had fallen into a dream.

Darkness descended. Complete, eternal, wonderful darkness and it permitted him to rest his brow. Lena was beside him. Cora, Baker, Ruth and Frank paraded in front of him as part of the staged revue. They were all there, bigger than life, smiling faces and welcoming hugs. His biological mother was nowhere to be seen, which meant she still lived. Strange that I should feel such joy, he thought, as he joined with his people and moved away.

11

It takes only a moment, Louise thought as she looked around the small room in which her father had lived, and none of the preparations you believe you have made matter at all. She had wept all night now, and it changed nothing. He was gone. His laughter, his rancor, his pure and unresolved anger, that thing that kept the fire burning in his belly and gave his life meaning, had gone with him.

She drove the distance from the city to gather his things. On arriving at the Home, she walked along the long dark corridor to his room. Her heart felt as if it would burst as she moved through the door and stood beside the high bed. Momentarily, she paused and looked around the room. Her eyes began to burn as she gazed upon some of the numerous objects her father had left for her. She could almost feel his presence.

Louise slowly began to remove the framed shiny photographs of herself and Wallace and Christine and George and his grandchildren in Philadelphia from the wall. She gathered his clothes, and finally removed his prize from beside the door. Touching the large photograph, she felt the electric jolt of his living energy. Like some fantastical play, an array of images flooded her mind and took her breath away. She sat down on the edge of the bed.

"Hello," the First Nations woman stood at the door and grinned. "You must be Louise!"

Quickly standing, Louise looked with mild surprise at the woman, and the despair she was feeling just a second ago dissipated as if blown away by a cool, insistent breeze.

The woman stood about four and half feet. Though she was not a tall woman, her body was strong, and she stood firmly in the doorway, accompanied by a mop and a pail of water at her feet, casting a shadow from the window light. She wore a piece of plain sack cloth as a dress.

As the woman's round, happy-looking brown face continued to glow, she turned briefly to look back down the corridor. That's when Louise saw the tiny jade carving of a turtle clasped to the single, long, newly-oiled braid trailing down the woman's back. She was clearly the cleaning lady. And, yet! In the years her father had lived at the Home, and she had visited him regularly, she had never seen the woman before.

"Yes," Louise replied. "Are you new? You knew my father?"

"Oh, yes! My name is Sohi." Leaving her mop and pail at the door, the woman strode quickly across the room and grabbed Louise's hand. "Sohi Lavallee. . . . I am Ojibway. . . . Oh Yes! We knew your father. Yes! He visited us quite often. Did he ever tell you about his time in the Arctic? He did his first vision quest with us. He was a holy man. . . . Your father was one of us. It is not every day that you see a black man do what your father did. Before he joined with the Great Spirit, he asked us to talk with you. He said you would need our help."

Louise looked at Sohi as if she were envisioning a glittering light, a thing that was so different from what she had known. She had met with First Nations parents on many occasions. This woman, she thought, is different. 'Your teacher is on the way,' her father had said in the dream. Momentarily, she was sure that Sohi knew her father far better than she herself did.

"Thank you, Sohi," Louise smiled as she shook her head. "I never knew that my father had done a vision quest. I don't even know what a vision quest is! Lately, though, I am seeing many things about my father that I never knew."

"Don't worry," Sohi laid her hand on Louise's arm and looked up directly into her eyes. "We will help you. Before I must go -- I am supposed to be working right now. Ha, ha! I'm just here for the day. My sister got sick -- I want to invite you to join with us as we visit with the Grandmothers on Sunday mornings. I will call you with the details you will need to find us. Bye!"

As abruptly as she had appeared, Sohi was gone. And Louise could not help herself. The woman had said that her father was a holy man. What a thing! She grasped this new reality, this new discovery, with an almost giddy happiness. This too, she thought, is a part of his legacy.

She placed the remaining clothes and other artifacts he'd left behind in one of the cardboard boxes she'd brought. She paused for a few moments when she'd completed her task to explain to the receptionist that someone was coming for the heavier stuff, like his chest. And she said goodbye to those staff members she'd come to know. The feeling of separation, of finality overwhelmed her as she loaded the boxes in the car and took one last look at the Home.

The drive back into the city was far less anxious. He was gone now. During all the talk and the tears and the organizing for his memorial, she had not quite accepted that he was gone. Until now, and she breathed deeply.

Images of the little Ojibway woman floated before her eyes as she drove through the shifting scenes of the afternoon highway. She recalled how clear and vivid the moment had been. How startling it was that there had been no pretense in their meeting, no facades. There were so many occasions, when on the first meeting there is a silent clash, an awkward and uncomfortable moment. Not this time! This time, everything was plain and simple and shrouded in a new kind of mystique. She knew that it was her own sense of wonder that was going to propel her forward and she had little choice except to follow, to go wherever it led her. Sohi had come to her with a message and a purpose. Sohi, Louise mused. Was she the "teacher"? She would speak with Wallace about this. Of all people, he would know what a "vision quest" is.

12

Wallace never knew when it all became so political, when so many other voices joined in and uttered the same cries. "Something has to be done".

As he looked around the long, wide, shiny oak table in Heddon Hall's large conference room, his eyes fell upon many familiar faces, faces of people with whom over the years he had shared other professional endeavors. Now, along with Louise who had accepted Tom Yates' invitation and who now sat at the far end of the table, more than a dozen social scientists and professors from other universities sat together in the spacious room and they all nodded in unison that something had to be done.

Four months after the initial discussion with Tom Yates, this first meeting anointing his dream project stood officially convened. The dean had issued the invitations shortly after their talk, and a week ago people began arriving on campus from a high-end mix of Canadian and American universities.

Wallace acknowledged that developments around Yates' proposed plans were moving swiftly. All the previously planned forums, focus groups, seminars and an array of other activities were now enacted. Other buildings in other locations on the campus were also welcoming people from other parts of the country. Many other people began expressing the same concerns Yates had talked about. Only a few people were hesitant to speak about their fears.

"Is there really a possibility that another civil war can be fought over something like this?" Alicia McRoberts, who sat beside Louise, taught courses in Social Justice at the University of Ohio. Her state was recently under media scrutiny over the death of another child at the hands of law enforcement.

"Those who are unaware of human history risk much," Dr. Perry Scarf said. He taught history at Lehigh University. With his elbows on the table, a thick lock of his graying hair hung down over his forehead and partially obscured his glasses. The man's long fingers were entwined and folded together his chin. He spoke directly to each of the people who listened to him. Behind the spectacles, Scarf's blue eyes were like ice.

"When law becomes lawless," Scarf continued, "those people who must live under it get upset. How many times have we seen populations pushed to the brink by unfair laws, watched themselves be slaughtered, and decide to fight back only when they can go no further and when it's often too late? In a space of a hundred years we watched two different peoples in two different parts of the world, driven by the same needs, and with two different moral and nationalistic visions, fought back and overturned systems of oppressive government founded on the aristocracy and the arrogance of wealth. I say that if we do not do something, people here will also begin to fight back."

"Above all else, my friends," Wallace responded. "We must continue to respect law and order. The last thing we need is another civil war. Besides, our anger will only exacerbate the problems. More people will suffer and die. No. I am convinced that we must approach this thing with calm intelligence."

"You are right," Dr. Scarf said. "When you read and teach history, and you see repetitions of the human tragedy over and over, darkness descends quickly. All of this begs the question: just how long has it been happening here? Though many people have heralded it, why are we only now awakening to it? Nowadays, it is more than one group of people who are being persecuted, and we are all aware of that fact."

"Yes," Dr. Yates intervened. "I agree with Dr. Briggs. The reason we are brought together is to find solutions that will prevent any further violence. We don't call for revolution. We call for reform."

"Yes," Wallace nodded. "And with reform there are sometimes almost impossible challenges. For instance, how do we bring reform to something as rigid as an intractable mindset taught by the centuries to view anything or anyone that is different as just that, 'other'?"

"There's the rub!" Yates grinned. "That is the distinct reason for our being here today. I'd wager that finding the answer to that one question would provide all of us with more relief than we can imagine."

"First," an olive complexioned young Hispanic man with brown eyes and a razor-thin moustache sat straight up in his chair. "First," he repeated. "Let me introduce myself. My name is Ortega Ruiz. I am a Sociology Fellow at the University of Pennsylvania. Again, first! I speak for myself and for other people who share the same faith and who hold similar views. In other words, we believe in God.

"Over time, however, we have seen other influences creep into human consciousness and attempt to displace God. Generally, those influences have been largely unsuccessful, and we have survived. There is a new problem on the horizon. Right now, many of us need to understand how it is that law enforcement has become more powerful in our lives than is our God.

"So many people, including and especially our children, are living their young lives in fear. For multiple reasons, to be sure! When we pray to God, we pray out of love for the beloved Father. We pray for protection from the many evils of this world. Though the response is not always immediate, the faith of our fathers brings happiness to our hearts. Also, and most important, our God does not arrest us. Our God does not beat us up or shoot us in the back and then plead innocent of any wrongdoing. Or, God forbid, deport us all back to the places from which we escaped. I believe that none of us in this room today have played a significant role in creating this alternate God. Yet, here it is. And we cannot rid ourselves of it."

"Not without a fight, anyway!" An unidentified masculine voice lifted into the air.

"Who said that?" Dean Yates' face reddened. "Why do they always talk about fighting?"

"Go with it, Tom!" While Yates was at the head of the table, Wallace sat at his right hand. "Some people need to blow off steam. Hear, hear!" Wallace grinned and clapped his hands and nodded his head toward Ortega Ruiz. "I'm sitting here, Wallace continued, wishing you folks had met my father-in-law."

Wallace looked at Louise who smiled back him as she stood up from her chair.

"Hello, everybody," she said. "I am Louise Briggs, and I am deeply honored to have received an invitation to be here with you today. As a high school teacher, I feel a little out of my depths. However, listening to the conversations about the rough times we are experiencing has lifted me to new heights. I also believe the concerns expressed here are valid and right on the mark. For me, this is all a true gift. So, thank you all." She reclaimed her chair.

Wallace breathed deeply. He was sure that his wife's timing had rescued him from his own anxiety. Still, the thought of Henry being in the room with them nagged at his own consciousness. As an educator, he reasoned, isn't clarity of thinking as important as critical thinking? He missed Henry. He missed driving out to the Home alone, unknown to Louise, and sitting for hours playing chess and talking with the old man, his daughter's beloved grandfather.

Now, as he sat in this conference room and listened to people from other parts of the continent speak with the same intensity as did Henry, Wallace was amazed. How, he asked silently, can one human being have perceptions that simultaneously stretch far back over time and reach knowingly into the future? Somehow, Henry had managed to connect the links.

It is February now, he thought. A new year, 2015 Anno Domini. Henry is gone, of that he could be sure. They had done his memorial, for which even his brother-in-law had travelled from Philadelphia. They spread his ashes in the place he had chosen. For a while, though, he had worried about his daughter and her reaction to Henry's passing. He feared that her mental stability might suffer. He had still not forgotten what happened when she was only five. Then, one morning at breakfast, Christine had startled both he and Louise.

"I saw Grandpa last night," she said casually over her bowl of cereal. "He told me to tell you that he is fine and that you are not to worry about anything."

All reason had not deserted him, as he had thought. He still felt some small bit of regret for not being completely honest with himself about Christine's health during that time. Then, something magical happened, and though nothing was ever said about it he had known instinctively who Henry was. How many times and in how many places had he encountered men and women who were like Henry? And they were all healers.

Her tenth birthday is only a few days away, he thought. I mustn't forget. I must make it an especially festive birthday for my girl. What does a ten-year-old girl who has never been fond of dolls want for a present? He would coordinate his own efforts with what Louise had planned.

There is much to do before that date, Wallace thought, and most of it is right here on this campus. He was busy. In addition to his classes and his participation in other research projects, the new head of the Coordinating Committee was frequently on the phone with him. He was also playing second host to the people already crowding the school's campus. Right now, Dean Yates was beginning to explain his project to the people who were gathered in the conference room.

"Our task is to become chefs and make a pot of soup," Yates said. All the other eyes in the room were on him. "In order to make the most savory soup, we need a variety of ingredients. . . . We have formed a coalition with other schools, and we all agree that we will give this project a christening, a moniker. We are also in agreement that we will call it "The Human Project". There can be no question that our purpose is anything other than anthropological.

"To undertake this project," Yates continued, "and working closely with your respective schools, we have established the fundamental foundation from which we are able to identify our goals. Our mission statement is clear and purposeful. We will be working toward a comprehensive understanding of what lies beneath and gives endless buoyancy to human endurance and perseverance during times of difficult life circumstances. Our researchers have determined that people who do not possess that buoyancy have much shorter life expectancies. In the end, we will be asking each of you to return to your own communities and set up storefronts and workshops. Question the populations about their concerns and their hopes and dreams."

"Dr. Yates," Alicia McRoberts called from her seat beside Louise. "Will there be some reward for those people who participate? I mean the people we will be speaking to."

"Yes," Yates responded. "Provisions are already being made. However, I must advise you right now! This is not a plum job. You will be opposed. As has happened on numerous occasions in the history of higher education, universities and their students have always been in the vanguard of social change. They have also been the recipients of authoritative wrath. Who can forget either Kent State or the Orangeburg Massacre? You must expect that there will be anger, sometimes even violence. Still, emphasis must be placed on those people who are living under the yolk of poverty, and who are being persecuted by such institutions as law enforcement.

"Who would attack us?" Dr. Scarf had removed his glasses and his eyes blazed.

"Since we now know that the predatory terrorists who have always lived amongst us, and who are alive and well and living amongst us still, we will need to be alert at all times. The information we seek is there, often buried deep in the subconscious of each of the people we interview. We must question both the realities and the rumors of what is happening in the lives of those unfortunate people who are stuck in a world of lack, and who live forever below the poverty lines. Discover how they are dealing with the various stresses in their lives. Most important, however, it is time to discover and identify who or what it is that holds final responsibility for the distressful conditions lived in by so many people.

"Please understand that ours is a singular purpose. We do not enter into this endeavor as if it is a fool's errand. Nor are we proposing any kind of ideological platform. We are not seeking any kind of revolution or the creation of a socialist state. We are, however, after removing inhumane and unfair barriers to human progress. That means establishing equality in every tier of human endeavor. We must find ways to not only refute the early teachings about equality. We've all heard these tired old arguments about how none of us are equal to one or any other person, and we know how these views are spread. Now we must also reinforce the positive meaning of the word 'human'. Knowing this, we must try to discover if it is even possible for opportunity to exist for he or she who is not prepared for it? If not, find ways to prepare them, even to the point where they can create their own opportunities. As I am sure everyone knows, these are the goals that organizations like the Peace Corps have always sought. This time, we are forced to acknowledge that the necessity for these goals lies at our own doorstep.

"So, you see, my friends, ours is a big job. But it is a job that is long overdue.

"On this topic, we believe that some of us in academia can no longer play ostrich and hide our heads in the sand. I am sure, based upon the chorus of voices I've heard, that each of us in this room agrees that we must do something. We must participate in ways that only we can. Therefore, I say again. It is a big job. Perhaps the biggest we have ever undertaken. But that is our raison d'etre. Isn't it?"

"Where is this intended to lead us?" Dr. Scarf asked. "We are all aware of where we are, and of how we got here. Neglect, I believe is the word. Neglect of each other and of ourselves. Geez! That ought to be a slogan on a decal. . . . Is this our 'Come to Jesus moment'? If so, what is at the end of the road?"

"Dr. Yates," Wallace interjected, "I'd like to take this one." Rising from his seat, he looked at Yates and waited until Yates nodded his head. "Thank you."

"Dr. Scarf has voiced the essential question," Wallace said. "Thank you, Sir. . . . I will try to be brief. Before I start, however, I would like to tell those who need to find the restroom, please do so now. As a matter of fact, why don't we all take a 10-minute break. When we return, there is much more for us to discuss and to concern ourselves with. This may also give you a chance to review your own questions."

13

"Grandpa," she asked, "why are these things happening?" In the dim light, she had trouble seeing his face. His entire form was simply not clearly visible. Nothing, however, stopped the child from asking her questions.

"Because we are human beings, sweetheart," He answered. His voice was little more than an echo, coming from some faraway place. "And we make many mistakes. But there are ways to avoid most of the friction, and you don't have to worry. Your mother and your father will be there for you when you need them. Just like your old grandpa. Remember now, that you are very precious for all of us. In time, you will know that you must be alert, and that you must learn all that you can. Keep your eyes open. Promise me that you will do that."

Before she could respond, he was gone.

14

Minutes before the break was over, everyone attending the conference was already back in their seats.

"As everyone here knows," Wallace resumed his oration. "there are many issues that we academics look at through only the lens of cold, hard facts. Depending upon our fields of focus, that is our nature."

"At times, however, when what we are examining affects us on a personal level, it is hard to maintain that stoic objectivity. What *is* at the end of the road? The truth about it is that I can't speak for other people on this topic, even using this compilation of statistical data I have managed to collect and which I have at hand. Perhaps that is because it simply isn't enough to just be aware of the whole array of concerns that each of us is feeling about the world we live in. And, of course, this leads to the next most obvious question: what can we do about it?

"At this time, however, my own objective goals are still subjective thoughts and feelings and I can speak only for me. The question that Dr. Scarf asked has tugged at my own thinking processes for a very long time, and the con- clusions I have reached arc very likely to change in the future. Right now, the 'end of the road' for me is the basic guarantee that my child will live free of fear. Her children will live a happy and productive way of life.

"We are an educated group of men and women in this room and many of us have also been granted exceptional lifestyles. By that, I certainly don't mean to imply that we are financially wealthy. But wealth happens in all kinds of ways. There are many people who believe that knowledge is wealth. That is debatable. I only know that not all people can or do live the way that I do, or you do, and I wish they did.

"For many, being born in the wrong race has meant that they still do not experience the opportunity to improve either themselves or the lives of their family members. Many never experience even the fullness of life. What it is that they experience mostly, however, is contempt from the larger world.

"If you are thinking that it is all relative, that people who live in other cultures, countries, and worlds already have far different lives from our own and are not really concerned about improving themselves, I would suggest we all take another look. Let me immediately assure you that, based on my own experience, people everywhere that I have been share with us a world-wide attitude. Family is as important to them as it is for us. In less advanced societies, and the people who live there are less dependent upon the sophisticated trappings and mechanisms we live with. Many people have managed to find a reasonable contentment with their lives. We here in the west have a different set of values, however, and we *are* talking about our own world.

"Our treatment of each other has brought us to the brink of another social cataclysm. Exclusionary perceptions, policies, and practices have denied us levels of education and insight that we are all direly in need of. Because of that refusal to grow, all of us are diminished and we lose."

"How is what we are planning to do going to change that?" Dr. Scarf asked.

"I believe in many ways," Wallace replied. "Please consider this! Other people, and this is something that seems to have become a general belief in certain communities, that in both Canada and the U.S. people are living under antiquated and particularized legal systems. The laws of today are deliberately created and enacted as if we still lived two centuries ago. We have laws on the book, they complain, which continue to deny certain people opportunity, citizenship, and equality. Again, because of the colors of their skins, many are born into this world as healthy and vibrant cripples. Their disabilities, however, come at a time when they are least expected and are mostly founded on the slippery rocks of an irrational and outlandish incarceration rate.

"My friends, at the risk of sounding like a crusader, I ask that you bear with me just a little longer. You see, what we are talking about is reform. We need reform in just about every institution where people gather, such as law. Especially law! Don't get me wrong! I know there are some very bad people who live among us. No one person, no religion, nothing has ever found a way to eliminate criminality or deviousness or greed or plain old mean-spiritedness from our world. I ask you: are prisons the right way?

"By now, we must all be aware that North America's prisons are packed to the brim with men and women and children whose lives are already over. On the taxpayer dime, the numbers of people inhabiting jails both north and south of the border just takes your breath away.

"Something is very wrong when we see that more than two and a half million of our fellow citizens are behind bars, often for very minor reasons! We have recently witnessed people die brutal deaths in these places for something as insignificant as blinking an eye, people who should never have been there to begin with. We all know that the sickness inherent in this system isn't caused by the individual; it is a part of the very fabric of which the system itself is made. Its etheric essence is to create laws which make it hard for human beings to breathe.

"I don't know about you, but for me just knowing this fact does not reassure me!

"That our civilization – and I use that word with tremendous caution -- has reached this point is something we must talk about. Maybe it is time that we consider alternative ways to deal with our fellow human beings. In truth, though, this prison problem is simply a reflection of something else: our own failure to act sooner! Now, it appears that we have complicated the job, and made it almost impossible to do.

"Look how lucky we are! We're not *in* one of these places! We also know that many people who inhabit these places have committed no crimes. Just like us! We know that! They are the victims of inconvenient truths. Wrong place, wrong time! Frame ups, nuisances! Racism! What moral alternative do we have except to call for reform? We know what happens in these places. In every single instance when a man or woman is sadistically murdered in any one of these prisons, a moral failure wraps us all in its angry tentacles and its stain is reflected on our societies. If we insist on believing that innocence lives, then we all *feel* its death on each occasion an able-bodied person dies behind bars.

"My question to you is twofold: do more than a few employers deliberately go out and hire ex-convicts without motives that are suspect and/or nefarious? Employers have histories, too. Can a man or woman who are or have been imprisoned go to the polls and vote to change those who hold power over his or her head?

"I think we all know that the answers to these questions are simple: No! And not even to the grave!

"This, my friends, is just another of the social institutions where I believe the dance of genocide is intertwined with other methods being used to terminate the lives of human beings. I know this is a tricky area for most people. History itself shows us that the very thought that people are being exterminated because of who or what they are just scares the hell of out of most of us. But genocide isn't just about the elimination of certain races or ethnicities. It is also about depopulation.

"On the pretext of bringing an end to crime while filling these prisons with millions of people who can no longer defend or support themselves, who cannot have a family life as it is painted to be, who cannot find the fulfill-ment that comes with a life lived as fully as possible, there occurs a hideous and unnatural culling of the mainstream population of any given society. It can also be established that not only do we put to death tremendous human potential, but we also plant the seeds for far more general-ized social unrest and violence.

"We here in this room have the chance and the resources to end this destruction. We can save lives. If we choose to! As Dr. Yates has stated, it is imperative that we find opportunity for the unemployable.

"Unbelievably, many of those who are slowly dying in the penal systems are much more strongly connected with and akin to the tens of thousands of homeless people living in fierce desperation on the streets of our cities and towns. That these circumstances are occurring suggests that we have forgotten who and what we are, while at the same time assuring us with unmistakable clarity that we are certainly not the compassionate animal we were once thought to be.

"For he or she who is facing death on either the cold lonely streets or in a prison cell, the results are the same. Millions of people right here in North America must wear a new and inhumane classification. They are all 'throw-away' people, people who were never really supposed to enjoy the benefits of citizenship anyway. They have always been marked."

"I'm not quite sure I follow you," Alicia McRoberts called from her seat further down the table. "In what way are people marked?"

"Well, let's try this one." Wallace responded, "I'd first like to thank those thousands of people fighting on the front lines against it, but I think all of us in this room have learned one thing. By now, and because this central experience is one that only a few of us have been able to escape, we all know that *poverty* alone makes common-sense values almost irrelevant, whether financial or otherwise. I would estimate that a good third of the student body of any of our schools would happily testify to this as certifiable fact.

"Poverty is a cosmic force, and if it has a redeeming grace it is that it is supremely indifferent. It is color blind. It cares not about gender. It serves all who are unfortunate enough to wear its banner in the same way: with deprivation and lack. It requires a deep and abiding and hungry fear, and it drives many of us to do our level best to avoid it.

"This is the intractable, crippling, *'marking'* social condition that has been the lot of millions of imprisoned and non-imprisoned people alike through time immemorial. Yet, in our world, the elimination of poverty is a convenient 'cause celeb'. Media and big named entertainers draw in millions of dollars with their efforts to bring *attention* to poverty. To get elected, almost every politician offers the world that worn out line of rhetoric about how he or she is going to bring an *end* to poverty. Of course, each of us here is aware that it is more than unlikely that such an ambitious goal will ever be achieved. The one thing we all know with certainty, however, is that poverty continues to mire too many of us in the hungry bogs of agonizing hopelessness. I'd wager that everyone here has the very clear understanding that in so many ways poverty itself is a prison. Perhaps it is the ultimate prison!

"Interestingly, none of the aforementioned conditions were created by the people who are most greatly affected by them. Without citizenship, you can bet that they have nothing to do with making the laws. They do not hire the enforcers. Imprisoned, they and their family members know only one way of life and that way is often steeped in the most restrictive poverty. So, what does that mean? It means that millions of people must now live their lives under a system of law that is absolutely alien to them. They have come to know the system as a thing that is created, controlled, and sustained by the institution of indifference.

"Many will tell you that that is the very essence of Law. Indifference! They will also say that every symbol of Justice in existence is blindfolded. Therefore, we should expect fairness. Do not believe it! Law, as with anything, is manipulated to the advantage of those in power. Penal laws especially, seem to have a diabolical way of swelling already swollen egos. With a thriving prison industry that attracts vast sums of money, how else can it be?

"Falling short of snatching away the life of an individual, the system as rigged does something worse than murder. It demeans and corrodes the very spirit of what it means to be human. This isn't good enough!

"So, you see, my friends! The grand scope of things we must do is saturated with variable objectives, still we must try. I know that it sounds childishly idealistic in a rigidly realistic world, but at the end of the road, we should not have to work so hard to be human beings. We will have learned enough to move into the future without many of these awful encumbrances we must deal with right now. In an effort to answer Dr. Scarf"s question, I believe that at the end of the road, we can all take a bow and know that we have done the job for the benefit of millions of people. I hadn't anticipated turning this into a long-winded dissertation, my friends. For that, I apologize. Thanks, everybody," Wallace grinned and sat down in his chair.

Everyone in the room joined in the applause for Wallace.

"Well said," Tom Yates smiled his approval. "That is precisely the kind of passion we will need most for this thing to work. My friends, there is clearly much more to talk about, including the logistics of our endeavor. For now, however, let's take some time and go have a good lunch. Wallace, would you join me?"

"Of course," Wallace said.

"I guess now is as good a time as ever, my friend," Yates said. "I promised that if you agreed to help us with this, I would have some news for you," Yates continued as they followed other people through the exit. "But first, are you still up for this?"

"Well, judging by what we have done so far, I think so."

"It is February now," Yates continued. "Sometime around the middle of June, working with Ortega Ruiz and Dr. Snalda McDonald at the University of Pennsylvania, we need you to set up shop in Philadelphia."

"My goodness," Wallace grinned. That's convenient!"

"Pardon?"

"It's Louise's home. She was born there. Members of her family live there."

"Oh! Will that pose a problem?"

"No," Wallace shook his head. "I don't think so. My brother-in-law and his family will be happy to hear this. He's been begging for us to come down there for a few years now. His wish is coming true!"

15

Only a few short years ago, Louise thought, this land upon which I stand was beneath twelve feet of water. The spring thaw and the mighty Red River, swelling far above and beyond its banks, drowned many miles of this verdant countryside, this farmland. This land does more than just feed us, though. It is a sacred land, a historic land. Here, in this place, I can feel the spirits move. I can hear the ancestors speak. They remember. For thousands of years, human feet have trod upon this land.

The confluence of the Red River and the Assiniboine River, she remembered from a textbook she once read, did a wondrous thing for this area of the world. By producing a delta where trade and transport lifted the people of those early years and gave their lives a progressive arc into the future, the rivers played a lasting role in the social development of the area. Archaeologists are still finding relics from those early days. With every benefit, however, a payment was required. While they were the absolute source of the new wealth, the rivers were unpredictable. A flash storm could bring havoc and immense destruction.

Now, only the sun hung in the blue noon sky. A cool breeze swept steadily across the small clearing where the cluster of buildings and the large tipi stood. Around the perimeter of the clearing, the countryside was a delightful mix of early spring blooms. In the distance, other cleared fields and thick forests stretched far across the horizon.

Wearing her thick, hand-made red and green sweater, Louise stood quietly, her arms folded across her upper stomach. She listened to the surrounding sounds of the day. Over by the big Lodge house, children laughed and played games with tiny stones and sticks. Birds chirped overhead. In one of the far fields, a bull lowed. She tried to remember the number of times she had stood in this exact spot and looked at this exact scene and felt that she had come home. In the nearly five months since Henry's death, she'd come to the Lodge every weekend.

She recalled that first Sunday as if it were just today. That morning, not unlike this morning, just as she finished folding the first load of the week's laundry and was preparing for the drive, she understood that she needed Wallace to be in on whatever it was that was happening. After all, he was her partner in crime. Yes, she had thought, the time has finally come to explain to him what was going on.

"When I paid my last visit to the Home to pick up Daddy's stuff", she said to him as she sorted another load of dirty clothes and put them into the washing machine. "I haven't mentioned this yet, but I met someone else at the Home. A First Nations woman! Her name is Sohi Lavallee. She identified herself as Ojibway. Anyway, she told me that she knew Daddy, and that Daddy had done a vision quest with them a long time ago."

"A vision quest!" Wallace began to laugh. "I knew it! That old dog! How could he hide that for so long?"

"Well," Louise continued, "she also said that Daddy was a holy man. Before he joined with the Great Spirit, he asked them to talk with me. He told them I am going to need their help. I don't know what any of this means, Wally!

"I do know, however, that something is happening inside me. I am changing. Is it just my age? I don't know. I don't think so. I feel these changes on deep and unexpected levels. These days, I see those dreams I've always had very differently than I once did. I used to think they were something to be afraid of rather than something to be heeded and used. No more! Shifts are happening in my own personality – healthy shifts, I hope. But shifts, nonetheless! I feel them. And I'm not afraid. Almost everything that happens to me now seems larger than it ever was before. You don't think I'm losing it, do you? Should I be scared?"

"No," he said softly. "There is nothing to be afraid of. It seems you have inherited much more than you knew. Let me tell you a little bit of what I know about 'vision quests'.

"It is a very spiritual journey," Wallace said quietly. "People do vision quests when they have specific questions they need answered or desires they need fulfilled. It is usually a journey to gain insight into one's own life and experience. It involves purification in the sweat lodge, not eating anything and not drinking anything over a period of four days and four nights and living out in the bush all alone in a holy place during that time."

"Really?" Louise quizzed. "It sounds challenging. Doesn't it? But I wasn't thinking of that. Not yet. . . . Wait a minute! Do I understand you to mean that Daddy went through that process?"

Pausing just long enough to see him nod, "Oh, my goodness!" she cried. "I'm probably never going to be satisfied until I know what he was doing. What was he looking for? Oh, Wally! How could this be happening? I am a middle-aged high school teacher. Sometimes, I feel that I've always been a middle-aged high school teacher. Right now, though, I feel like Alice about to go down the rabbit hole!"

Reaching over, he pulled her close to him. His arms wrapped snugly around her waist.

"Anyway," She looked into his eyes. "Sohi has invited me to her home. I will be gone most of the day, because it's quite far. How do you feel about that? Wally, something tells me that I have to do this."

"Oh," Wallace said, the pupils of his eyes enlarged as he looked at her. "One of the reasons I love you is because you're an adventurer. Just like me. Let me be the first to encourage you to follow through on this. I have some ideas about it all, too. You know? I knew about Henry a long time ago. I just didn't have the details. No one else seemed to know either, because he didn't talk about it.

"You are his daughter, and I understand that you must do this. Just be careful. That is a world you don't go into if you're just looking for a playground. In the spirit world, a sacrifice of some sort is often required. If there's anything

I can do, you let me know. Meanwhile, I'm sure Chrissy and I will find plenty to do to keep ourselves busy today."

Following Sohi's directions, Louise had driven the fifty miles from the city into the flat, vibrant, living countryside. The highway sliced through long miles of thick forests, open fields, and briefly along the edge of the river. She reasoned that the number of farms she passed was just too many to count. By the time she reached the Lodge, she was exhausted. It had been a much longer drive than she had thought it would be. Sohi met her at the car.

"There was a lot of talk that you might not come," Sohi had said, grinning. "I'm glad you did, because I wanted to see Henry again. I believe you possess Henry's strength and power. . . . Come, you need to meet everybody. They are waiting. We have much to talk about. There is much for you to learn, and quickly! But, let's eat first."

She had moved with Sohi into the Lodge house and was surprised by the number of women already sitting at tables throughout the huge room. Each of them turned and watched and grinned as she and Sohi walked toward their own table.

"We are all sisters and cousins and aunties," Sohi laughed, "Just one big ole awesome and happy family!"

Everybody in the room burst into laughter at Sohi's comments.

"Come, Louise, you must meet the oldest woman amongst us. Her name is Snow Owl, and she has lived a very long time."

The old woman's hair was thinned and iron grey. Her face was creviced with age. Louise knew instinctively that it was the woman's eyes that spoke, that laughed, that wept, and were half covered with cataracts. Still when the old woman looked into her own eyes, Louise knew that she had been seen on a level more deeply than anyone had ever done. Then Snow Owl grinned, exposing bare gums except for a single tooth jutting upward toward the roof of her mouth. "Eat some bannock!" she said.

From that time onward, each of the women in the room that day spent time with Louise. Each of them showed her things that even she had to acknowledge that she needed to know.

She recalled those days when she was still a child, and she and Grandma Cora had walked through the fields outside of Gettysburg. Grandma Cora knew more about plants than anyone. Her gardens, both vegetable and flower, flourished under her energy. She had even healed people of a wide variety of illnesses with the medicinals she grew in her gardens. Louise was a full adult before she knew that her grandmother was Choctaw. Now, depending on the weather, she and Sohi trekked into the forest and out onto the fields, talking of the spirits, studying plants, studying rocks.

Each Sunday, Louise had made her way along the long highway and through the changing countryside to Sohi's home. She had smudged herself with sweet grass and crawled into the sweat lodge to spend time with the Grandmothers. The hot stones crackled, and she soon found that they were more than just hot. They were alive, and they drove pure energy into her body. They burned away a lifetime of acquired physical and spiritual poisons.

She felt that she had been touched by lightening, and that her soul had begun to sing. She heard the drum. She smelled the sage and the sweet grass. She heard the elder call forth the spirits. She felt the Eagle's wing touch her head.

Sometimes, she took Christine with her, and she was pleased when her new friends fed and honored her child in ways that she herself had never thought to do. Christine, after all, was Henry's granddaughter. And, of course, Christine had loved every minute of it.

"So, this is where you hide?" Sohi called as she approached Louise quietly from behind. "Right out here in plain view."

"It is so lovely here," Louise said softly.

"I have brought you something," Sohi said. "I know you must leave us soon. But I think you'll be back. Next time, we'll get you ready for your own vision quest. . . . Here is one of my going-away presents." Sohi extended her hand and dropped a small shiny stone in Louise's hand. "That place where you will go, that is your birth land?"

Louise nodded. "My brother is there with his family. My mother died there. Thank you for the gift. What is it?"

"It will protect you in your travels. You are worried?" Sohi asked.

"I'm afraid so. For such a long, long time there has been so much violence against black people down there. . . . It is hard to imagine that it is over by any means. Before he passed, Daddy was very worried about his grandchildren."

"Yes," Sohi nodded. "We talked about it. He under stood that the tentacles of that kind of menace reach far and wide. For a very long time, both your people and my people have been trying to find the rationale behind all this. You had to endure centuries of slavery. And you made them wealthy. In many ways, you were luckier than we were. They just about annihilated us. Now, when the spotlight is on us, I cannot help but wonder how it is that we, the first people, have lost so much! There does not appear to be much rhyme or reason or clear thinking or even morality used in the past. It was all just another free for all, and it carried a life or death urgency.

"Those residential schools were really just concentration camps for so many of our people, you know. It was either kill us or assimilate us! We were forced into those places, often at the point of a gun, to be made into something we were not. 'It's the law,' they said. But it wasn't our law. After a while, it was almost laughable for us when white people acted like we were the animals. The abuse and the pain they inflicted on us was something we were not prepared for. We did not understand when our brothers and sisters and cousins vanished into thin air and were never seen again. We did not know that it was even possible to rip apart a child's fundamental understanding of who they were. Cultural genocide and all that! There can never be enough shame heaped on that institution, and the people who gave it life.

"Snow Owl frequently talks about how we all lost our minds during those days when they took the children away. After that, many of those who managed to survive those prisons could not live. A terrible sickness lay on them. Alcoholism, hopelessness, suicide, and the very violence they were taught in those horrible places they eventually visited onto their own families. It wasn't long before we began to realize that all of this was just another part of the planned extinction of our people, which was proven over and over by the contemptuous rhetoric spit out of the mouths of the newly arrived Europeans, even as they were destroying us. It is hard to understand that kind of hate, especially since it appears to be based on greed. Often, when I find myself feeling low and miserable, I surprise even myself by laughing at this folly.

"Now, just to prove we're not crazy, we must try to do things different. We're always in negotiation over some land claim in traditional territories, or better housing on the reserves. There have been times when even our own leadership has let us down. When things looked like they are being taken completely out of our hands, we have marched and blocked roadways to have our treaties recognized and to protect our lands. The marches have not always proved fruitful. We don't always accomplish our goals. In those few times that we are successful, it is at a cost. Do you remember Oka and Ipperwash? Every now and then, there are tussles with the police and the ugliest face of humanity is revealed to us. But we remain active anyway. To honor our dead, we must do it. Just like your people!"

"Yes," Louise sighed. "You are right! For centuries now, it's been the same. So many people have died violent deaths. What for? Was it just to teach them that they are lesser than others? Was it just to show that they were destined to experience an inordinate degree of pain before they died? The only answer I can find is that they died because they wanted to live life more fully, and because somebody else, somebody with stronger weapons, was always there to crush such ambitious thinking and to help them along their way.

"Sohi, I can tell you this. My biggest sorrow is that my own mother was taken from me so soon. All my life I have felt incomplete. Her blood courses through my veins, and I would like to have known her. I like to believe she was a wise woman, and that she would find answers where I never have. Now I fear, and I pray that I will see my own child live in a changed world, a calmer world. You know what I mean?

"Daddy warned me to be on the lookout for danger where she is concerned. With all the stuff going on down there, I can't be sure any of us will be safe. Still, I am going. I won't stop looking for that calmer world, at any time."

"Oh yes," Sohi smiled and gestured her arms out in front of her. "I believe you do have a big job in front of you. That is what Henry said, and that is what I know. Somehow, if we are to truly honor Henry, we're going to have to find out how to bring that kind of world into existence. Aren't we?"

16

Much to his surprise, the week following the mid-June launch of The Human Project in Philadelphia exceeded Wallace's wildest expectations. It was immediately apparent that Dr. McDonald and Ortega Ruiz had been busy. All the legal hurdles had been cleared. Thanks to social media and some local media stations and newspapers, thousands of telephone and on-line inquiries were keeping growing teams of people busy. Throughout the state, places of education and places of worship, people were volunteering to work with the Project. In Philadelphia, storefronts were opened throughout the city in those areas where the many poor were concentrated. Maybe it was just out of curiosity, he reasoned, but a widely diverse line of people was streaming into the offices from the streets and signing up for the workshops.

The final display, the one about which no one had mentioned even a word, was certainly one of the best of the welcoming events laid before them. Dr. McDonald had also managed to find a comfortable rental house for the Briggs family for the duration of their two-month stay.

As it happened, the two storey house was just two blocks from the North 18th Street homestead where

Louise's family had lived for many years. Grandpa Avery was gone. Aunt Mary was gone, but George and his family now occupied the old place. Already the two families had joined together for the first outdoor bar-be-cue of the year. It had seemed only right that it be held at the place Louise had lived until she was sixteen.

Wallace watched with his own rising curiosity as Louise looked wistfully around the rooms she had grown up in. He knew that she had returned to Philadelphia on just a few occasions since her grandmother's death. After the funeral, she had gone north to find her father. At times, he thought, she appeared almost overwhelmed by her memories. He didn't quite know how to console her, but he stood beside her.

Christine also faced the difficult choice of either putting her father's birthday gift away and cease texting friends back home or getting to know her cousins better. She chose the latter, and now only occasionally did she communicate with her "bestest" friend Mabel, a young First Nations girl in her class and with whom she had formed a confidante type friendship. Now, however, she and Lucy, George's twelve-year-old daughter, were fast becoming friends. And the three boys! She didn't ignore them. They were all older than she, and she quickly put it perspective. Well, they were boys. That's all.

During the first few days after their arrival in Philadelphia, Wallace was besieged with telephone calls, meetings, and visits. Community leaders and clergy from every denomination appeared unannounced at his newly established office on Claremont Street. Wallace sensed their curiosity. He read the questions on their faces. He patiently explained who was involved and what he and his team was doing. He went on to let them know that it was a group of international universities which were officially embarked on an anthropological study called The Human Project. "It is a project that is of, for, and about those people who must live out their lives below the poverty line. We are looking for ways to lift them up."

"Of course," he said to a diverse group of clergymen one afternoon. "When I speak of study, I should add a bit to that so that it is not misunderstood. I am a cultural anthropologist. A portion of my job involves observing those activities, dreams, and influences that tend to drive a people either backward or forward. For instance, I already know that in this community and many others, the church is not only a cultural focal point. It is a driving force.

"For centuries, it has been the church that has centered the black community here and elsewhere. In doing so, however, these sanctuaries are left exposed and vulnerable. The terrorists who have existed since slavery often violate the soft sanctity of the church with violence and death. I want to first acknowledge the tremendous courage it takes to just keep on keeping on. Please accept my sincere admiration for what you have already done. I would also like to offer our help in whatever you may need."

He watched them as their facial muscles began to relax. He heard their almost silent sighs of relief.

"Both your reputation and the media has done you a big favor, Dr. Briggs!" One of the collared clergymen with short peppered hair and light skin stepped forward and extended his hand. "I am Bishop Lionel Franks. We knew you were on the way a long time ago. Thank you for trying to bring our communities into the light."

"Just what is it you're planning to do here?" One of the black preachers stood on the far side of the room with his hat in his hand. "My name is Reverend Miles Latimore. I am pastor over at Trinity Temple Baptist Church. I don't mean to be impertinent, but we've had numerous incursions into our community from a wide variety of sources. They all brought bright promises with them, and they all left with our world remaining much the same way it has always been. There's one thing that I think we can all agree on: we know where we are, and we know where we stand. What will you do that will bring a difference?"

"With your help," Wallace responded, "I am hoping we can bring a significant difference. My team is divided into different specialties. We have a mix of lawyers, sociologists, psychologists, and an award-winning film crew which is prepared to go to work immediately. In view of the long years of discomfort between the black community and law enforcement, I am hoping you will be forgiving enough to work with certain members of law enforcement, because we have requested their assistance in ways that are other than racking up an arrest rate.

"You know your communities far better than I do. I am hoping you will help to introduce us to the people. We need to talk with the people. We need to hear about them from themselves. On the first-hand information we obtain, The Human Project will be building a data base which is to become the springboard toward significant social change right here in this and other communities."

"I've seen some of the television documentaries you've produced, Dr. Briggs," Reverend Latimore stated. "Your acknowledgement of the problems our churches face cannot go unnoticed. But that is old news, and a very old problem. Been around forever! It is the lack of gainful employment for our youth which is most worrisome for us.

"Our president is doing all he can with 'My Brother's Keeper'. But it's not enough. And his time in office is almost up. After that, from where many of us stand, we are acutely aware that it is possible that we may be going back to the way we were, the way we have always lived: standing by and watching as the idleness guarantees the continued violent deaths of our children. If you can find a way to put an end to this gun violence, you will have achieved the miracle we all need. If talking with our people will help you do this, then I am with you. As their minister, I can speak for some of my people, and I will certainly speak to the rest of my congregation about the things you have said."

Watching as several more of the men nodded their heads and prepared to leave, Wallace breathed a sigh of relief. He had not thought it would be easy to sell the project. From immediate appearances, however, he silently acknowledged that his own uncertainty was laid to rest. He was delighted by the thought that Tom Yates' legacy project was gaining some legs. Now, they had only to collect the data.

17

"I can remember that both of us use to fly away whenever Daddy began one of his long talks." Louise said. "You remember? Who knows why we did it? Maybe some deep-seated anger! Took me a while before I could accept what he used to say about the dreams. I almost went crazy trying to prove he was wrong. Well, I'm here to tell you that much of what he said is true. He was bigger than we knew. Into things we couldn't have dreamed of."

"Well, Sis, are you going to leave me hanging or are you going to tell me?" Looking directly at her face, George arched his eyebrows. "Did you know about this at his memorial?"

"Yes," she said quietly. "I couldn't really talk about it then."

While it was a beautiful warm summer afternoon outside, the three of them sat in the cool renovated living room of the old house on N.18th Street. Anita was squeezed in snugly beside her partner on the giant sectional sofa.

Looking around the room, Louise remembered what it had been like during the time when she had lived here with Grammie and Grandpa Avery. It had always been a comfortable room, she thought, always just a bit out of synch with the changing times and fashions.

Now, Anita had come. And the woman had applied her unusual decorating and designing skills to the whole house, and she had turned this room, especially, into a spacious and luxurious chamber.

The front of the house was completely changed. The woman had eliminated the front bedroom upstairs and created a cathedral ceiling for the living room below. Gone was the single large window that looked out onto the street. The entire front wall was a series of tall tri-paned windows that reached from the floor to the bottom edges of the arch overhead. The silver sectional sofa was soft and compelling. An abundance of indoor plants cleaned the air and added fresh fragrance to the room. Amazingly, with four boisterous teenagers around, the place exuded an unexpected peace and harmony.

"I know one thing, anyway," George injected. "Change isn't always good. Change never alters the truth, and appearances alone are always deceptive. Between you and me, Sis, time and distance has changed nothing. Remember us? We were just a couple little waifs that nobody seemed to want. My big sister and me! No mama, no daddy for years until you went and found him. We're more than just blood. We're survivors. It's kind of funny that you mentioned the dreams earlier. I've been having a few of my own lately. In my way, Louise, I loved Pops more than even I knew."

"Just to give you a for instance," she said quickly. "I've met some people recently who knew Daddy. Some of them have said that he was a holy man."

"What? You're kidding, of course. My Pops! Holy!"

"Somehow, he found redemption", Louise added as she watched the look on her brother's face bring back memories from their childhoods. They had been born only a year apart. With their mother dead and their father gone, they had leaned on each other, relied on each other in the way all siblings do when it is just themselves. Their grandparents were there, but that just was not the same.

Her brother was older now, as was she. Like her own, his eyes were widely spaced. The differences she saw now were that his eyes also carried a vision of sadness, and slender streaks of gray had found prominent places on his head. And, unlike herself and their father, George had become quite stocky. "It seems he really did choose to walk along that path less traveled. He was a healer, my brother."

"All that Voodoo stuff gets me all jittery," He replied.

"It isn't Voodoo! And even if it were, it wouldn't be a bad thing."

"No," Anita finally joined into the conversation. "I think Louise is right. Didn't I hear you say it was First Nations people? Traditional? Wow! That's a whole different kind of spirituality! In so many ways, its message is about healing, and about achieving oneness with the sacred earth!"

Louise looked at her sister-in-law with a new and startling pride. That the round-faced happy woman who had settled her brother down, an action which itself had to involve exceptional healing skills, had also kept herself current was no great surprise. She stood no higher than five feet, and she was a plump powerhouse of energy. Louise smiled. That's the reward for bearing and raising four children in this world, she thought. You just don't have time to stop. In Anita's case, there was more. During the years of raising her children and solidifying her family, she had also become a professional chef.

"You know, Louise," Anita said. "We hold these, for lack of a better word, discussion nights over at the church. Not prayer meetings! Just little get together meetings to talk about what's going on in our world. Yes! You can believe that after Charleston, we're all on alert. There are people who patrol the area from six o'clock in the evening to six o'clock in the morning.

"You can see how it is that so many of the things happening here and around us are leaving indelible and unforgettable impressions on all of us. Especially, the children! Even here, our hearts are still heavy because of what happened at 'Mother Emmanuel'. Before that it was Newtown where one unloved white child went crazy and murdered all those other tiny sweet children. And some adults! But the same thing has always been here! Always! And we black mothers are always feeling the same deep pain that the mothers in either Charleston or Newtown felt, and still feel. We all understand now that every time a child is murdered in this country, a hole is left in our hearts. All of us! This kind of emptiness is not refillable.

"Right now, and right here, we are all under siege and it isn't another upset child who is attacking us. It's those who are supposed to protect us. We're being forced to watch them murder our children, and ourselves. And get away with it! The good Lord only knows how much time any of us have left. By now, everybody must be talking about "Black Lives Matter", even up in Canada."

"I would hope they are, but I have my doubts," Louise said. Her recent intimate experiences had taught her lessons that often left her feeling less than enthusiastic about a whole array of things. The egoistic uncertainty that often comes with illusion had been stripped away from her by the white fires of the sweat lodge. Now, except those closest to her, she no longer saw or accepted anything without silently questioning.

Thinking of her friend Sohi back in Canada, she paused. After all the bravado, all the trumped-up patriotism, she asked, is there a nation in this world that is without either current or historical social blemishes? So far, she remained unaware of any place where all people were treated with respect and fairness.

"On the whole," she said, "I think Canada has other problems to deal with right now. But, you know, I'd be happy to join you in one of these meetings. Let me know when, and we'll go. We'll take the girls. By the way, what church is it?"

George turned his head and looked at Anita. In turn, she paused and looked down at her folded hands. Then, as if relinquishing a treasured secret, Anita nodded.

"It's Mama's old church." Hooding his eyes, George turned back to Louise. "Trinity Temple. It's still our church, Sis. Just like it was when we were kids. Anita's in the choir. All the kids were baptized there."

"You have to see it, Louise!" At the mention of the church, Anita's voice resounded with excitement. "After all these years, we've managed to regain and restore some of its history. Lena Throdmore, your mother, is now officially recorded as one of our most outstanding leaders. Like so many other women throughout our history, she gave up everything for the cause."

For a moment, Louise simply leaned back in the big easy chair she occupied. Again, the air around her was thick and impenetrable as she silently acknowledged the internal conflict that had haunted her since her childhood. Yes, she thought, she gave up everything for the cause, including her life and her children.

There are always surprises, she thought. Over time, the often and silent questioning of her own confusions about her mother had left her feeling numb. How is it possible to adore someone you have never known, she quietly asked of herself? Now they honor a long dead woman who just happened to have been our mother. How are we supposed to feel? Am I supposed to be overwhelmed with phony gratitude? Daddy, God bless him, would be proud as Punch. I, on the other hand, must live only with the shadows of what might have been. Still, I suppose it is a nice symbolic gesture, and I will try to honor it.

"I'm looking forward to going," Louise smiled. "It will be nice to see reality. This, after all, is the reality I know better than any other because I grew up with it; not the one skewed by either my job or the media to favor the status quo.

"I'm trying so hard to understand why any of this is still happening! Didn't we go through a long overdue social revolution sixty years ago? Isn't that what the Civil Rights Movement was all about? Didn't our mother die fighting for the same things we are fighting for today? Can it be that there are still attempts to deny us even basic human rights? It's almost unbelievable that here we are in 2016, with a black president, and it's only recently that much of western media has begun to acknowledge that black people just might be human beings. That's some progress, I guess!"

"No, Louise," Anita cried. "It's not! All my life I've had to deal with those people who repeatedly refuse to *see* me. For them, I am just another black woman, a welfare queen, as they like to say. I am just another unimportant nonentity. How many times, even as a child, have I heard them say: 'Well, black people just want to be accepted.' Even my early educators, some of whom were white, happily planted this harmful thought into the minds of the children. From the beginning, my question has been the same: accepted by who?

"No, my sister, it's just too hard for any of us to go through a day without either hearing about or witnessing the murder of another black man or black woman or black child by the police. Right now, even though I'm supposed to know that my three boys are right out there on that basketball court and my Lucy is upstairs with Christine playing computer games, all safe and sound, my heart rate says otherwise. My hands feel sweaty. It's like I'm just waiting for that dreaded phone call. If, for lack of anything better to do, we could all just curl up in a ball in a corner somewhere and cry ourselves to death, we would achieve about the same as we're getting right now – nothing! You can bet your bottom dollar the system is not going to give us anything.

"You speak of human rights. I've heard that up in Canada you guys have a Human Rights Act which is supposed to protect people against discrimination. Is that true? Does it work? Down here, we have a whole bunch of 'holier than thou' politicians who just love mounting their moral soapboxes and pointing fingers at other nations on the pretext that we're somehow better than they are. Look how easily these liars toss out words like 'exceptionalism' when referring to this country. What crazy talk is this? We're not exceptional! We never have been. We're just people. High and low and in between, and we all go to the bathroom the same way.

"You know, Louise, maybe it is even unreasonable for any of us to expect that a nation founded on the enslavement of human beings, the greedy and undisguised genocidal slaughter of tens of thousands of indigents, and which remains persistent in its persecution of minorities to have any respect for human rights, let alone be exceptional!

"Do you remember the lawyers who were there with the families of Trayvon Martin and Michael Brown and a few others who have lost their sons and their daughters? Where are those guys now? Why was it so impossible for them to get justice for those children? I certainly don't believe that it was because they were incompetent.

"Just so you know, we mothers at the church ask these kinds of questions, Louise. I don't always think we'll get answers. None of us do! But we've learned definitively that we cannot expect to be given anything, not even the lives of our children. They kill us with impunity. That's all. That's it. Nothing more!"

Louise was stunned by the frankness with which Anita spoke. Her sister-in-law sang the dirge, the song of death, as easily as she breathed. Louise had heard it before in other places and at other times, and she was more than familiar with the kinds of conditions that evoked the hymn. She also had to admit that the same thoughts had crossed her own mind, many times. Even her dying father had warned her. After everything, she was a mother too.

She was thankful to the alarming influences of media and her own innate understanding of history, and she was keenly aware of the many unnatural deaths in this place where she was born. Many times, when she thought about her own child, she felt the fear rise into her chest and almost take her breath away. How could a race of people survive this kind of unending onslaught, she heard the question rise from her belly.

"You remember that old song, Sis?" George laughed. "'It's the condition our condition is in'. When I came back down here, I didn't think it would be this bad. We've all lived with it our whole lives. You know that! Even when Pops was a child, the lynchings touched our own family. I don't know why I thought I could be all cool with everything. On this score, I should have listened to Pops.

"After what happened up there, I just wanted to forget. The most confusing time of my life involved coming to understand that, in many ways, it is the same there as it is here. I guess I figured that the only escape was just to work and do what was needed. Pops gave me that ethic, you know. I got lucky. I got old, and my kids can go to college. My main job now is just to keep them alive and out of the way of the police long enough to do that!"

Suddenly, Louise felt very tired. Why, she asked silently, was there always so much uncertainty, so much fear? Where is my 'calmer world'? Looking across the room at George and Anita sitting awkwardly on the edge of the sofa, she was shocked as the two figures quickly diminished to the size of small dolls right before her eyes. She felt the silent prayer begin in the pit of her stomach. She felt the prayer's energy move over and begin to rise up along her spine. Help me, she called, and instantly she saw another possibility.

"You guys!" Leaning forward, Louise shouted jubilantly. "You know, there is another reason we're here with you this summer. Wallace is working on a project here. It's my understanding that he is looking for just the kind of first-hand stories we have here. He makes documentaries, you know. He also has a film crew. In some circles, their work is very popular. With a bit of persuasion, we might just be able to get him interested."

18

"Mama," Crouched on the sofa in the living room of the rented house with her legs folded across as if she was meditating, Christine fidgeted with the ink sketch pen she held in her right hand. Then she paused and looked at her mother, "when are we going home? I miss Mabel and my other friends."

"In August, Baby," Louise answered, "just like we planned! What's the matter? Are you feeling well? Aren't you having a good time with your cousins? You seem to enjoy being with them."

"It's not that. It's nothing, Mama." Unknown to the child, Christine's face was registering a very different story to her mother.

"You just wait," Louise smiled, "we're going to have a grand time. It's Independence Day next week! Just like Canada Day back home! That's always a good time for having a lot of fun, isn't it?

"You know what? When I was a girl about your age, I lived here. Your uncle George and I grew up in the house where they live now. And every 4th of July the people in the neighborhood threw a block party. We had so much fun! There was lots of music and dancing in the street and food! Everywhere you turned there were long tables over-flowing with food, and people were eating and laughing and having fun! Then there were the fireworks. They were pure magic. I am told that they still do the block party. And the fireworks! You want to see that, don't you?"

"Yeah, I guess." Shrugging her shoulders, Christine appeared even more listless and less interested.

"What's the matter, honey? Talk to me!"

"Mama, all the kids are afraid of something! What's the matter with them? Nobody can go anywhere alone. Nobody wants to play outside! Or go for a walk to the store! You must always have another person with you. I don't understand."

"I know you don't, honey. I don't either."

"Did you know that Lucy is a singer? She is good, Mama. Really good! She told me that she sings solo at the church every now and then. Lucy is going to perform with some boys on the 4th. I'd like to see that! She's the next hip-hop queen! I love hip-hop. I want to be a singer, Mama. I bet you didn't know that either."

"No, Sweetie," Louise replied. "I didn't know that. This is the first time you've said anything. But I bet that you would be a great singer! You have a beautiful voice."

Finally, the girl smiled. "Thank you, Mama! When we go home, I want to take voice lessons. Can I do that?"

"Of course, you may. And it's 'may' I do that, not 'can' I do that! If you still feel this way when we get home, Daddy and I will find you a good teacher. But let's figure out what we can do before that. How do you feel about coming with me and Aunt Anita to the church this evening? Your father's film crew is going to be there and he's going to interview some people on camera. Lucy is coming, too!"

"Will she sing?" Christine asked.

"Maybe, if we ask her to. So, what do you think about that?"

"Okay!" As Christine grinned and returned to the picture she had been drawing, Louise retreated to the bedroom for a short nap.

19

Venus gleamed in the evening sky. An occasional tailed ball of fire streaked across the wide darkening horizon overhead. Beneath it all, multicolored flowers rose up high off the night earth and exploded in startling blooms. The ooohs and the ahhhs of the crowds below were swept away like tumble weed by the westerly wind.

She stood in the middle of it all. In the crowd, among those she knew and those she did not know. She understood instinctively that it was their imagined understanding of patriotism, of belonging, that boosted their joy, their laughter, their celebration of some past event in distant time. And it rang out like the screams of a newborn infant.

Even through the massing waving weaving throng, she saw him. An aura! A child! She heard every muscle in his young body scream as he ran toward her. She watched his mouth enlarge as a gaping hole, desperately trying to pull in the air that would keep him alive. He ran! He ran! At first, it was only the sounds of a backfiring car that surrounded the boy. Then she saw the four men running behind him, panting, pointing their guns, firing their guns!

A long collective scream broke the air as the boy drew nearer to her and the first bullet pierced his back and exited his chest, spewing blood and tissue in all directions. With his hands reaching to the sky, the boy stumbled, fell, and did not rise again.

The crowd closed in. Around her, the festivities of the evening screamed on without pause. She wept.

20

Descending the stairs into the cool basement sanctuary where the deacons and the sisters of Trinity Temple Baptist Church held important meetings and taught Sunday school, Louise caught her breath as the flood of emotional memories from her childhood rushed in and absorbed her thoughts. Of course, she hummed, Grammie was with me in those days, and everything was as light as air. Though Anita had spoken of changes, the room in which she now stood was very much the same one in which she had spent so much of her early life.

Everything was as she remembered. The same musky odor of age, the same giant gold-plated cross she had adored as a child still hung against the wall in blazing contrast to the crimson colors surrounding it. The slightly raised tiny wooden shelf underneath the cross gleamed from a recent polishing. The only difference Louise could find was that now the large room was aglow with imported lights. Members of Wallace's film crew moved about in a hurried frenzy of activity. A diverse collection of people had gathered in one corner and were talking excitedly.

"There's Reverend Latimore!" Anita announced with an almost giddy loudness. "Louise," she continued, "you have to meet him. He's our pastor."

Louise saw the pastor, but she also spotted Wallace in the increasingly crowded room. Waving to him, then she pointed him out to Christine. She watched as the girl immediately pulled away from the two women and, with Lucy in tow, weaved her way through the crowd until she stood only a few feet from him. And he saw her!

She saw him grin, reach out to Christine and pull her close to him. Though she was out of earshot, she watched Christine nod her head eagerly in response to whatever it was he was saying. Then she saw Lucy trail behind Christine toward the rows of chairs reserved for them all.

"Come on, Louise!" Anita grabbed her arm and pulled her toward the man she wanted her sister-in-law to meet.

"Reverend Latimore," Anita called out. "I want you to meet Louise. She's Lena Throdmore's daughter!"

"Oh, my!" For a moment, the man seemed startled. Standing almost six and a half feet, the Reverend's slender body was clad in an aged and worn dark blue suit. He also wore a white shirt and black tie. Gray hair covered the man's entire head. His eyebrows were gray. His dark face looked tired and yet he appeared as a man who had just emerged from a long nap. Louise sensed his strength and his pain. Several of his teeth were missing, but he did have a gold tooth. And when he grinned, that gold tooth shone in the light like a tiny miracle. As he reached out and grabbed her hand, Louise was suddenly overwhelmed by the very personality behind the face.

"Lena Throdmore's daughter!" The man gasped. "My, oh my! I am honored to meet you. Even though I wasn't here then, your mother was one of our treasured jewels."

"Thank you, Reverend." She replied. "I am happy to meet you, too."

"We must talk," Reverend Latimore said as his eyes were pulled in another direction. "Forgive me. I am needed somewhere else right now. We must talk." And he hurried away.

"How did they reach so many people?" Anita asked as she looked around the room.

"I believe it's a pretty big network. Lots of universities involved," Louise replied as they moved toward the rows of chairs where Christine and Lucy waited. "And there's always word of mouth."

The crew had transformed the sanctuary into a studio. Power lines snaked in all directions across the carpeted floor. Three separate cameras on tripods were positioned strategically around the room. A small, oval, newly erected stage against the north wall shone underneath the overhead lights. On the stage, two cushioned arm chairs stood opposite each other with a small table between them.

Before long, the rows of chairs where Louise sat with Anita and the two girls were all occupied. Other people had arrived, and soon the air was abuzz with whispering voices as if they were at Sunday morning worship, where speaking too loudly would somehow offend God.

Then Wallace, followed by an older white woman whose very appearance screamed for attention, stepped onto the dais. The short thin woman was accompanied by two children, the smallest of whom was a girl who could not have been more than six years old. Holding on to the little girl's hand, the woman sat down then lifted the child onto her lap. The other child, a boy who was already a teenager, wore an angry and miserable expression on his young face. He sat down on the edge of the stage, bowed his head and waited.

All three members of the little family wore soiled, multicolored and multiple layered clothing that seemed glued to their bodies. The woman's graying blonde hair was unkempt and appeared to not have been washed for many days. Her eyes were frightened. Her face was a jumbled collection of small scars and splotches. Even before she spoke, Louise knew that she and the children were homeless.

Louise began to feel a growing discomfort as she watched the scene unfold in front of her. Reaching over, she wrapped her arm around Christine's shoulder and pulled her closer to her. From the corner of her eye, she saw Anita do the same with Lucy. Then she heard the cameras click and whir into life. Seconds later, the first interview began.

Looking directly at one of the cameras, Wallace began with an introduction. He quickly explained what they were doing and what they hoped to achieve with the film they were making. Then he turned to the woman who sat opposite him.

"Would you tell us who you are, please?" Wallace asked softly.

"My name is Ella Moore," the woman replied.

Louise immediately surmised that the way in which she spoke did not match her appearance. She sounded as if she had received a higher education in some other place and at some other time. Somehow her life had fallen into tragic circumstances. She watched quietly as the woman tightened her arms around the girl on her lap.

"These two are my grandchildren, Josh and little Sarah." Ella Moore continued. "Thelma, my daughter and their mother, died from an overdose of heroin six months ago. Their dead-beat father, that useless freak, hasn't been around for years now. Nobody knows where he is. I guess he wants nothing to do with any of us.

"Anyway, we were alright for a while. We had a little trailer over near the park. It was an old thing and not in the best shape. Leaky, you know. But it was home. Then we lost that. After that, everything just got to be too much. We had nobody or nowhere to turn. Even welfare cut us off. Well, you know the rest. We've been on the streets ever since."

"Can you tell me how you heard about us and what we are doing?" Wallace questioned.

"It was an accident," Ella responded. "We came out of the shelter one morning last week. . . . Some nights we can't get into the shelter, but when we do we gotta walk pass the old York theater. You know the one that they closed and locked up over on Wright Street more than a year ago now. People sleep under cardboard boxes in the alleyway by the building. At times, we've had to do that too! Sometimes, in the early morning, the Salvation Army truck is there, handing out coffee and sandwiches.

They don't even ask you to pray. Last week, Josh found the paper hanging on the street light pole next to the alley. The paper told us where to go if we wanted help. We went. Eventually, we wound up here."

"How have you managed to hold your family together?" Wallace queried.

"By the grace of God," Ella replied. "Child and Family Services have been trying to catch us. They want to take my babies away from me. If they do, I will die. If something does happen to me, I pray that some good people will look after them. Right now though, as soon as we hear that CFS is on the way, we light out. . . . I want the best for them. I just don't believe foster care is the best for them. Nobody else can love them the way their granny can love them. Until something changes, we'll just keep on hiding. Yes, it is hard. But after all these months, we're still alive and we're still together."

"If we can, what do you want us to do for you?" Wallace continued questioning.

"I don't know what you can do. I hope you can help keep my family together. I am getting old, but I can still work. And I will work. I used to work as a paralegal. Right now, that all seems like such a long time ago."

Listening quietly to the ongoing interview in front of her, Louise began to weigh the significance of the moment. Again, she thought, here it is! The illusion and the mystery mingled together in an interminable exhibition of human misery. How can this be? I wish I had not exposed my child to this, but she does need to know the world she inhabits. And this too is a part of that world. She needs to understand that there is tremendous variety in life, including the highs and the lows. She needs to know that some people experience challenges which make life just another horrible dance between the susceptible and the vulnerable.

What better teaching tool is there, she silently questioned herself. She was acutely aware that the song Ella Moore sang on the stage is being and has been sung by a chorus of thousands, tens of thousands, who were also unresisting and wounded. She saw that there are things which appear so simple, so inelegant, and so profoundly unforgiving. She acknowledged that even she, but for a twist of fate, could so easily occupy the chair opposite Wallace. Nothing was altered, and it could be any woman! Or, man, for that matter!

Still interviewing Ella Moore, Louise noticed, Wallace's questions were a bit sharper. She wondered if he was nearing the end of this first interview. She also wondered what they would do for the woman, if anything. That was the greatest unanswered question, and this was the moment when the truth had to be revealed. That is the hinge, she thought, on which everything depends. It has got to be more than idle talk. It's got to be edible, functional, touchable.

For a moment, she watched as Wallace looked around the room. Then, as he looked toward herself, she could see that he saw the look of question on her face. He turned back to Ella Moore sitting opposite him.

"Ms. Moore, you have provided us a lot of food for thought this evening. In this city, you are our very first interview for the Human Project. Thank you! We cannot permit you to leave us without showing our gratitude. One of my associates, Mr. Ortega Ruiz, is waiting to talk with you. He is aware of your situation and has made some arrangements for you and the children. Before you go, know that you are not alone. We all know how easy it is for any of us to misstep, to forget the dangers which confront us daily when we stand too close to the abyss. I often think that the real tragedy is that so many people have lost their footing, have stood too close to the edge and have fallen. We are here to help you regain your footing and to get you back up again!"

21

Looking out onto the street from her seat on the front porch of the rented house, Louise suddenly felt that she needed to go home, back to Canada, back to the life she had built there. Christine had spoken of it more than a week ago. While she could not concede to going too soon, she had managed to calm the girl down with promises of what this holiday would bring. But now it was she who felt the pull, and the only thing she could think clearly about was how different it would be when she got home. Her father was gone now. It had taken her awhile, but she had finally come to terms with how dependent she had become on just the sight of him. She missed him. She was sure now that he had deliberately held his entire life up in front of her as a giant question mark. He left the world with many grievances and many questions, she thought.

Henry was gone, but there were still so many other things that strengthened her purpose, things that would make her rise from her bed in the mornings. For the first time since their arrival in Philadelphia, the teacher inside of her began to stir as if awakening from a long nap. Questions, almost impossible questions, began to rise into her thoughts. And, too, she missed her students. She missed her classroom.

On this day, the Fourth of July, she saw only that she was far away from the place she had grown to love, from her house, and her classroom and what she now thought of as the 'sedate life' she lived. No, she mused, she was in the very place where the day itself held a special meaning, where each year, and for this one day, all things exists under the auspices of Independence.

Here, she thought, this is the kind of day that deliberately displays a nation's need to remember, to nostalgically acknowledge that implacable sense of something special, of liberation, and that almost religious sacredness which seems to touch everything. Yet, it is also a time to celebrate the more than two hundred years since the nation's founding. By all measures, it is a young country. When compared to some European and Asian countries, this place is almost an infant. And everybody knows how much the young loves to dream of impossible futures. Like impetuous youth also, some nations need to take the time to question what is most important.

In teaching, she thought, we convey so much information. We become such good and responsible actors in the societies where we live. Even armed with all this righteousness, however, an essential question lingers with us. Here, in this place, the Fourth of July is supposed to be a day, a twenty-four-hour period, which is dedicated to the idea of freedom! It is supposed to be about the thousands of men and women who fought so hard and died such horrible deaths in the name of sovereignty, in the name of liberty, in the name of freedom. What do I say to my students when inevitably they ask this fundamental question? What is freedom?

I will say that it is an imaginary thing, Louise thought, a thing to be dreamed of. Or, maybe it is a state of being. Maybe, it is being absolutely unencumbered by attachments, attitudes, expectations, restrictions, and illusory deceptions. The magnificent paradox, she laughed silently. There is a stressful futility in this never-ending pursuit of freedom. The pursuit alone is a narcotic. All prisoners want freedom. All slaves want freedom. So, who has freedom?

The standard definitions of the word offered by the dictionaries leaves much to be desired, Louise thought. There are too many variables. The word itself seems to have different meanings for different people. Based on those definitions, the word is a balance between what is good and what is bad. There are people who believe that it is their God given right to have the kind of freedom that permits them to do harm to other people, to control, to oppress, to murder. And, yet, there appears to be a unity, an implication at least, of a blessed 'state of being'.

That is what this day, this Independence Day, is supposed to be about, she thought. That metaphysical state of being! It is that place where the imagined imprisoned are liberated, where the shackles of bondage are removed forever.

Leaning back on the cushioned lounge she'd placed out on the porch, Louise breathed deeply. She felt rewarded by the afternoon sun wrapping her in its warmth. Christine was with Lucy at the old homestead on 18th Street where Lucy was getting ready for her public debut as a young hip-hop queen. Wallace was busy editing the recent "Ella Moore" video they had recorded. Gazing out onto the afternoon street, Louise people-watched as passers-by nodded and waved to her.

Her eyelids became heavy as she looked toward sky. The expanse was deep blue with only a few scattered and small clouds. She luxuriated in the lazy comfort she felt, and she listened to the sounds of construction over on 18th Street as people readied themselves for the upcoming street party tonight.

Finally closing her eyes, she instantly felt the familiar drift begin. She slept.

. . . A long collective scream broke the air as the boy drew nearer to her, as the first bullet pierced his back and exited his chest, spewing blood and tissue in all directions. With his hands reaching to the sky, the boy stumbled, fell, and did not rise again. . . .

Louise abruptly felt that wrenching shock of displacement as she awoke from the dream too quickly and found that the contentment of the day had already vanished with astonishing speed. Her heart was beating much more rapidly than she had previously known, and she felt fearful anxiety grip her entire body. For the second time she was visited by the same dream. That had never happened before. There must be a purpose, she thought.

The dream lay on her like a hot blanket. She tried to push it from her thoughts, but it was impossible. What is happening, she asked silently. Sitting up and inhaling deeply, she felt the alarm rise into her chest like a flailing hammer. What else can this be but a warning? I've got to be careful. 'Vigilance' is what her father would say. 'Be vigilant!'

Christine! Where is my child? She looked at her wrist watch. It was 6:30 in the evening. Still startled by the dream, she found herself even more surprised at the amount of time she had napped. Loud music was already reverberating through the air, floating over the rooftops from 18th Street.

Louise quickly gathered the things she'd brought out onto the porch and took them inside. She was acutely aware that she was moving faster than usual as she rushed into the washroom to refresh herself. A few minutes later, she locked the front door and walked quickly toward Trinity Temple. She would meet Wallace there, she thought. Christine and Lucy would be there. Anita and George would be there.

The entire section of the street where the church sat was blocked off. A makeshift stage had been erected on the street about fifty yards from the church grounds. Already, a couple of the musical instruments, a trumpet and a trombone, gleamed in the waning light as the players sent their musical offerings resounding sharply through the air.

Louise saw that along both sides of the street, long tables held up an assortment of pastries, smoked ham, roasted chicken, and other tasty delicacies. Many people were already there, and the mix of voices was becoming more and more raucous. With their cheeks bulging, neighbors ate, drank, and slowly began dancing to the music. To rise above the loud din of noise around them, people were suddenly laughing together even louder.

Louise stopped as she arrived at the steps leading up to the church's entrance. The full picture of the excitement surrounding her was a contradiction unto itself. Discordant, joyous! People were everywhere.

On the stage, a group of young men harmonized Jazz melodies from the 1960s. When a young woman with glossy black hair, sporting a huge white blossom, and who wore a silk off-white gown joined the group, loud cheers from the crowd lifted into the air and welcomed the young woman.

The music changed, and the woman began to croon a medley of old tunes that Billie Holiday had recorded generations ago. Louise stood entranced. This is my heritage, she thought. This is what I was born out of. For a moment, she was enthralled. She did not hear the doors to the church open. It was only when she felt the hand on her shoulder that she turned to see Wallace's smiling face. Reverend Latimore stood beside him grinning, gold tooth and all.

"Are you okay?" Wallace asked.

"I'm not sure," she replied. She silently acknowledged that one of the reasons she loved this man was that his sensitivity was finely honed. "Another dream!" she said. "If it were not the same dream that I told you about, I probably wouldn't feel this way. It almost never happens twice. Where's Chrissy?"

"The running child?" he asked.

She nodded. Again, she found warmth in simply knowing that since she had begun visiting with Sohi and the grandmothers at the Lodge, she and Wallace were much closer. She confided in him in ways she had not done since shortly after they met all those years ago. Over time, she began to more fully explain the dreams to him, providing as much detail as she could recall, and she was pleased when he had responded with an unusual and unexpected enthusiasm.

"Chrissy is still inside," he said. "Lucy is doing one last rehearsal. Chrissy is helping her. I didn't know that our daughter is an aspiring singer? She's quite good, too. . . . They will be out in a few minutes. By the way, we're going to film as many of the events as we can."

Louise nodded. "How are you Reverend Latimore?" Turning briefly from Wallace, she greeted the pastor. "I am happy to see you."

"You know," the Reverend's eyes gleamed as he responded to her. "We have a custom here at Trinity Temple. If you are the descendant of a former member of our family here, you are a member in your own right and for your entire life. I wanted you to know that."

"Thank you for saying that," she responded. "I spent a great deal of time here in my early life. Yes, my grand-parents. Wasn't here much during the time my mother lived though."

"From what I am told," the preacher continued. "You are much like her. She and Reverend Greene worked together to bring some important people here back in the day. They even organized some of the Freedom Rides down south. That kind of leadership is still needed today. . . . It does this old heart good to see that you and your husband follow in their footsteps. You have come here to help us. That's funny, isn't it? I almost wish I didn't have to say that. As a daughter of our church, you and yours should be here for only one purpose, and that is worship. . . . I understand you are a teacher up there in Canada?"

"Oh yes! I was thinking about that before coming here today."

"You sound like you enjoy it," the preacher said.

"Oh, I do! Each day is different, and loaded with activity. And I have a very diverse group of students. That makes it especially interesting for me. You'd be surprised by how much I learn from my students." She could not tell him that it was one of her students who had ushered in perhaps the most significant change in her spiritual life, a student who had brought her to that place where her father had tried to lead her for years and she had not sensed it. Standing here, she thought, in front of this church, in front of the past, where I have stood many times as a young girl, can I tell this man that I am walking a different path now? Can I tell him about my friend Sohi, and my father who left without my ever fully understanding him? Can I speak with the reverend about a new vision I have acquired? Not today, she laughed.

"I have always believed," the pastor said, "it is a blessing from God when we find our calling."

"I think you are right, Reverend," Louise smiled.

The doors to the church opened once again and the two girls, Christine and Lucy, skipped quickly down the steps.

Seeing Lucy dressed in a cherry red faux leather jacket, a low-hanging pink T-shirt, and a pair of very short, yellow hot-pants, Louise felt her anxiety vanish only to be quickly replaced by a joyful and wonderful picture of youth. Lucy also wore a tam that was angled over her left eye, and her lips had been painted a strawberry red. Louise laughed as she reached over and pulled her niece closely to her.

"You are a star!" Louise grinned. "Don't you ever forget that!"

Looking at her daughter, Louise saw the look of youthful pride and expectation on Christine's face.

"And you, my girl," Louise grabbed Christine and hugged her. "I see what you mean now! As soon as we get home, we'll start looking for a teacher for you. Okay?"

Looking up into her mother's face, Christine grinned. Her eyes gleamed happily. "Thank you, Mama," the girl said. "We're going over to the stage now. See ya later, alligator!"

She watched as the two girls walked quickly over to the stage and stood with a group of four boys who were all to play and sing with Lucy. The little group called themselves "Hood".

Louise glanced at her watch. It was 8:15. Overhead the bright sky was darkening. Soon the fireworks would begin. She turned to Reverend Latimore.

"Reverend," she asked. "Has there been much activity from 'Black Lives Matter' in this neighborhood?"

"Those children are a new line of defense for all of us," Reverend Latimore said emphatically. "They are deliberate, and willing to die. Just like we were back in the sixties!

I am old now and I am tired. . . . We have been struggling for such a long time. For centuries now, each generation of our people experiences the same thing over and over. They have enslaved us. They have lynched us. The list of our grievances is too long, almost unending. Now, they are murdering us openly on the streets and with impunity.

"Don't those who hold power over us ever get tired?" the preacher continued. "The only message I am able to give to my congregation is a message of hope. It is the same message we have been delivering for centuries. And it is a message that I repeat over and over. But deep in my soul I believe that there should be something more. A lot more! Right now, even though I know that the very words I preach often sound like they are mired in fear, I just can't change it to something more uplifting. Sometimes, I listen to what I am saying when I am preaching, and even I don't believe it. It's not just a crisis of faith. No, no. I can never lose that. But I can't help the dismay I feel sometimes. That's why I asked that question. Are they like the rest of us? Don't they get tired?"

"They do," Wallace said soothingly. "It's just that sometimes we have to show them that they are tired. You know, my job requires that I maintain an overview, a detachment. Sometimes I fail. As you may have guessed, Reverend, I am an advocate of "Black Lives Matter". It is as important to me as the air I breathe. It must be that way, because I have a lifelong investment in it." Looking toward the newly erected platform, he saw his daughter and his niece huddled together and he smiled. "From where I stand," he continued, "watching the unarmed and the vulnerable being continuously gunned down on the streets by people who are supposed to be looking out for them is just about unbearable."

Already a crowd of people were gathering in front of the stage. Among them, George and Anita stood waiting. Anthony and Louis, two of their teenage boys, were with them. Louise, Wallace, and Reverend Latimore walked over to the gathering and squeezed in near her brother and sister-in-law. The excitement on Anita's face as she looked toward the stage and waited for her daughter's appearance is just about contagious, Louise thought. George's eyes gleamed in the light as he simply grinned in anticipation.

"Child," Anita said, "I have been waiting for this a long time!"

"We all have," Reverend Latimore said. "As I just said to Louise, it is a blessing from God when we find our calling. This young child may well have done that."

At nine o'clock, the very first popping sounds announced the beginning of the fireworks display from Moses Park. Then, for some fifteen more minutes, the night sky was a garden full of bright flowers. Lucy and Hood finally took the stage, and the crowd cheered.

The music accompanying the little troupe was tight. More importantly, it had been created by the members of Hood. Like a pendulum, their individual voices drifted high and low. During their performance, Hood moved about the stage ceaselessly, back and forth, left and right. With their young voices like striking hammers against the night sky, the boys spilled a frenetic energy and excitement from their very bodies out onto the crowd.

Lucy stood in the center of the maelstrom on the stage, her red jacket shouting out at the night, her body moving rhythmically to the beat, her clear voice lifting and falling. Her lyrics were some of the most unique Louise could remember hearing.

Listening closely to what these young people were singing, Louise heard a mish-mash of energetic synthesis. Their lyrics screamed about the desire to live, "to be free of gun-riddled streets. No more drive-bys, they called. No more guns! No more killer cops!"

She is only twelve, Louise thought of her niece. My goodness, they are all tuned-in. Each of them is super aware of the world they live in. This is what Christine was talking about! Other children did hide fearfully in the dark. Whatever happened to childhood?

Louise was only mildly disturbed when, without warning, the fireworks abruptly ended. Yet, the popping sound continued. Somehow it was different, though. That internal alarm awakened again as she understood that whatever it was the sound represented it was moving in their direction. It is strange, she thought. It is intermittent. Now it is there. Now it is gone. And she couldn't determine with any certainty whether it was a backfiring car or something else. The partying people around her did not seem to notice anything.

Lucy and Hood finished their act with loud applause. Then all five of them came down off the stage and were replaced with another group of older musicians. One of the men carried an accordion in front him.

When Louise heard the popping sound again, it was much closer. She looked around to see where it might be coming from. Two blocks down the street, beyond the barricades that stopped all automobile traffic from entering this section of the street, she saw him. Only the streetlights sporadically emphasized the shadowy running figure.

Through the many people scattered here and there along the block where she was, she watched as the running figure drew closer. In the dim light, she could see it was a young boy. When his course suddenly veered in her direction, she knew only that she was locked inside a dream. She had to be! This could not be real. No, she screamed silently. Unknowingly, she grabbed hold of Wallace's hand.

"What's the matter, Lou?" Wallace's face tightened and looked seriously concerned as he draped his arm on her shoulder.

"Tell everybody . . . ," she tried to speak, but the words would not come out. If this was a dream, she needed to wake up. She was not asleep, but she could not wake up. The nightmare held her enchained. And the only escape she could find was to let whatever it was that was happening happen.

The popping sound quickly returned. She saw the boy again. Almost breathless, his mouth agape, the young man was just on the other side of the barricade now. With his feet pounding the earth to obtain maximum speed, he was less than forty yards from her when the popping sounds multiplied, and she saw the hole open in the boy's chest. She watched as his blood spewed out into the air.

Still, he was up and moving. He even managed to get past the barricade before he fell. Suddenly, other people in the crowd screamed.

A yard to her left, where George and Anita and two of their boys were standing, there was another commotion. Someone else had fallen. Turning her head, Louise peered through the diminishing light.

Anita was not standing. George was not there. Anita was bending over a prone figure on the ground. The figure on the ground was unmoving under the night sky. The two boys knelt anxiously and quickly beside their mother. Only Reverend Latimore stood tall, his gray head bowed as if he were reciting an incantation, his long arms hanging loosely beside him. The pastor looked down at the figure on the ground in front of him as if in mourning. His head moved from side to side, over and over.

"Somebody, please call a doctor!" Anita screamed, "Help!"

When she heard Anita's cry, Louise felt her own jagged panic rise into her chest. It is my child, she immediately thought. Where's Christine? Where's my child? She closed her eyes and did not reopen them. She could not bear to witness her child's death.

"Wallace," she heard herself shriek. "Who is it? Please tell me it's not our baby!"

"No, Sweetheart, Chrissy is right here with us. We're together . . ." He paused too long.

"Who?" Louise cried. "Who is it?"

"It's George, Lou." Wallace murmured.

"George? My brother George?" Hearing the agony in Wallace's voice, Louise felt her own body fall in on itself like an emptying bag from a vacuum cleaner. She felt the scream, still distant and more primal than anything she had known, form into a tight ball in her belly. She tried to breathe, but she could not. Then, as if she had just realized what she'd heard, that her brother had been killed right before her eyes, right in front of the church where they'd both grown up, she fainted.

In that far dark region, Louise could hear herself scream in agony. No! No, no, no! Where am I? How can this be?

When she awakened again, she was in Wallace's arms, but the very first thing Louise saw were the four police-men standing over the body of the boy they had killed. Did they know that they had killed someone else? Did they know? Did they care? She saw that when they finally heard Anita's cries for help, one of the policemen casually walked over to where George lay dead on the ground. Not bothering to examine the prone body of her brother, the man called for medical help. But it was too late.

Louise was already overwhelmed by that horrible sense of finality, of the unexpected and unwanted ending. She already understood the very essence of finality, that absence of senses. Never to be heard. Never to be seen. Never to be known. Six months ago, she had experienced it with her father. Now, she thought, it is my brother. Even through the pain, she gratefully allowed reason to break through into the moment. With stinging eyes, she stared through the dark at her sister-in-law huddled over

George's body. The only thing left to do, she thought, is to help Anita as much as possible while we're here.

She pulled away from Wallace and rushed to Anita's side. Dropping down beside her sister-in-law, she was immediately startled by the fact that it really was George who lay sprawled on the ground. He was not moving. No sound came from him, no moans, no groans. He was gone. Bending over her brother's body, Louise almost lost consciousness again.

In the night and with the mass of people surrounding them, she could barely see his face. Reaching down, she felt her shaking hands as they roamed over his unmoving body. His arms, his legs, his chest, all of it! She tried to find his pulse. When her hands found his face, she felt his eyes, his nose, even his still open mouth. Then she became aware of something else: she desperately needed to prove that he still lived, that it was just too hard to believe that he was dead! Her brother, the boy with whom she had grown into this world, the boy who had cheated death more than once before, was dead! No, she cried, not even his blood on her fingers could prove he was dead.

When the EMTs finally arrived and determined that he was gone and took his body away, Louise and Anita clasped their arms about each other, their bodies wracked with pain as together they sobbed the most bitter tears of their lifetimes.

22

Standing in the open doorway of his Claremont Street office, Wallace looked across the street where other storefronts were becoming active. Though it was early in the morning, people were already moving in and out of Hinton's local grocery store on the corner. The manager of the five and dime store directly in front of him finally opened his doors. Standing quietly, he listened to the revving motors of cars and trucks roar as they drove slowly past him.

Finally, he turned away from the street and looked around the large room where most of his activities occurred. He was still alone, waiting for his staff. The room housed the computers and telephones and radios his voluntary staff needed to keep things moving forward. Several location charts and maps covered with brightly colored pins hung on the walls.

He had been here for two months and a week now. In another week, he would be following Louise and Christine, both of whom were already gone. He tried hard to shake the sadness he felt. So often in his professional life, he had left people and places behind. Everything was always in flux, transition. Until he married Louise, he was unsure he would ever escape that feeling of instability. For years, his closest companion had been the utter impermanence of everything. Now, he was unable to pinpoint with any accuracy just which feeling was the heaviest. Sorrow, regret, relief, the missing element! He felt them all anyway. His little storefront had given him a reason to be hopeful. Here, he was able to do something different. His motivation was evident on the faces of the people who came through his door. The storefront was now a hub of tremendous, sometimes anxious, activity.

He recalled the time when he had had to admit that his job really did require a certain kind of personality, the kind of personality which allowed him to remain reasonably focused, sensitive, purposely detached, and unharmed. I am a professional to the nth degree, he laughed. He was sitting at his desk when the door opened and some of his staff strode into the room. He could hear them whispering to one another while busily occupying themselves with the daily tasks of readying the shop.

Wallace had long ago learned how to listen to his own thoughts, how to read and eliminate that often unending internal dialogue. There were times when he even had to acknowledge that, during his time in this world, he had accumulated a vast amount of life experience. His earlier travels alone had shown him unimaginable levels of humanity and fulfilled his boyish dreams of adventure in ways he might only have read about in textbooks.

Now he was drawing near to the end of his brief tenure in Philadelphia. He dismissed the temporary emptiness that always came with such departures and refocused his thoughts. With all the distractions, he had held his team together and they remained focused. He had also managed to complete his recordings. Seventeen new videos now contained much of the information he came here to acquire.

He knew that this was the end of only the first phase of the Human Project. Other people, in other states and provinces and under the auspices of the Human Project, were embarked on similar programs. From the information he had received, he sensed that each of the offices that remained open were enjoying a surprising success. Even this office will carry on, he thought. The results of all of this will eventually reach the university labs. The researchers will pour through every piece of the material with every resource they possess. They will pull information and conclusions from the gathered data that he and others were submitting.

Aware that there remained much to do, Wallace was still able to find reason to silently congratulate Tom Yates for what had been achieved so far. The man could retire, he thought, with an unusual level of grace. He congratulated himself, too. Somehow, he had managed to overcome all his early reservations about involving himself with the Project. Now he could only acknowledge the worth of the work he was doing. His videos had certainly brought a new and different perspective into his life. In many ways, he had reintegrated with his own humanity.

He could go home now. Once again, he could resume his life with his family. His wife and daughter returned home almost month ago, shortly after George's funeral. And he missed them.

Wallace knew that back home other interviews were in the offing, other documentaries. He knew, too, that with a bit of prodding, the Project would extend well into the years ahead and with a bit of luck could positively alter the lives of millions. We have had a good beginning, he thought, and we made some progress. There will be benefits, and memories. Many memories! The people in the communities with whom we worked, he would inform Yates, have all cooperated with the Project to the best of their abilities. They have freely supplied the cultural information we were seeking.

If only it could all be summed up so easily, he thought. If only the night did not have eyes and people did not die. Since his own father's demise, he hadn't contemplated what it would be like to be there one minute and gone the next. Even Henry's departure, which he was prepared for, left no illusions. He knew also that this one was different, that he would never forget the night when his brother-in-law died. The autopsy on George revealed a stray bullet from a police revolver. Somehow the missile weaved its way through a mass of other people and lodged itself in George's heart.

While he remembered the initial conversation he and Yates held regarding the Project, '. . . the demographics of the here and now,' Yates had said, 'the manner through which many deaths are occurring. . .' He wondered if he would ever be able to completely remove the recurring pictures in his head. Images from that night along with the memories of the surrounding circumstances plagued his thoughts. It had all been filmed, but he was still unprepared for the unexpected suddenness of it and it had jarred him to the core of his being.

Louise had been devastated. He had tried to comfort her, to find some balm that would end her pain. A near impossibility. In the end, he was forced to concede that he could not, that there was nothing he could do. He would also never forget watching Reverend Latimore as he stood tall and still over George's body. Even in the subdued light of the night, Wallace had seen the silent, silver tears of hopelessness trickle down the man's face. Wallace quickly understood how losing George had overwhelmed all their lives. How else could it be? In that dark moment, he made his decision.

If necessary, he vowed, I will devote the remainder of my time on this earth to the creation of other spiritually invested life and death recordings. When we dive into the well of thoughts, he reasoned, isn't that the fundamental human question? Life and death!

"The thoughts are there," Henry had said to him one afternoon long ago when he visited the old man at the Home. "They are the real proof of life and this ability we have to reason. I think, though, that it is essential that we look for the spaces between the thoughts".

23

The evenings were the worst. Each day, just as dusk began to settle around her, the ghosts came, and she was haunted by her own frightful memories. Even her dreams had ceased. After what had turned out to be an exhausting and agonizing four weeks in Philadelphia, Louise now found that being home still had not provided her the relief she so desperately sought. On some other level, perhaps even her subconscious, she knew that it would be a long time, if ever, before the images of that terrible night were removed from her mind. For now, she could not forget that it was her own hands traveling over her brother's dead body in a futile attempt to revive him, in a vain effort to believe that he still lived.

When all was said and done, she remembered too that it was the look of sheer terror on her daughter's face that night that finally brought an end to their trip.

They remained there until a few days after George's funeral. During much of that time, with her husband's compassionate understanding, she stayed and talked with her sister-in-law, Anita, for two more days.

Looking down at her ever-moving hands, Anita looked back at her sister-in-law. Her face and her voice were filled with nostalgia. She spoke of George and herself when they were both still young, when laughter was always in their hearts and on their lips.

Their conversations became increasingly intense, they spoke often of the unavoidable, about the traumatic shock suffered by the children who had witnessed the events of that night. Then Louise listened as their talks too quickly became a mixture of tears and fear. There were many moments when the two of them were downright inconsolable, when simultaneously, they mourned until their eyes flooded again, and their tears flowed unceasingly.

She recalled how her own daughter, Christine, had gone into a trance, and it had taken she and Wallace hours to bring her back. Her niece, Days after her father's death, Lucy, who only a few moments earlier had entertained the crowd that night, now spoke to no one and she could not end her tears.

At the end of their two-day session, she had had to inform Anita that she and Christine were going home. Her sister-in-law's response was almost predictable. Anita breathed deeply. Then she stated emphatically that they would all be okay. She quickly lowered her head before looking with teary eyes around the big living room.

"It's so empty here," she said, looking down at her tightly clasped hands. "I don't want to lay any kind of a trip on you. I just thank God that I still have the kids. And thank you for everything you have done for us," Anita said, her lips quivering as though she was having a hard time holding back her misery. "Of course, you must go," she finally said. "You have a busy and I would imagine a wonderfully different life up there in Canada. I know too that you must get yourself ready for the school opening in September. You just come back home anytime. With the good Lord's help, I'll be here." Anita paused. Then she said, "I envy you."

Lowering her head, Louise listened as she began to worry for the rest of the Throdmore family. She and Anita finally discussed how they were all going to survive. If they needed it, she could send them money.

"No!" Shaking her head, Anita quickly responded. "George," she added, "tried to set things up for any eventuality. Through his work, he had made provisions for us all. For a while, his insurance will cover our expenses while we wait. The family lawyer has already begun the wrongful death law suit against the city. We'll be okay.

"And I can always start cooking again," Anita had said finally.

Wallace remained behind to finish up the work he was doing, but he was with them at the airport. Christine walked beside him, her arm reaching as far around his waist as possible and she hugged him as tightly as she could. Louise saw the look of sadness on his face as she and Christine had moved through the loading gate, turned briefly, and waved to him.

As always, when she was home, she reached toward the familiar which had never failed to bring that different sense of belonging and peace into her life. She meditated continuously as she moved about the house, neurotically cooking, cleaning, checking herself repeatedly before she barked at her child.

If only, she thought, having a sparkling house could erase that night of music and wonder and the specter of death. If only I had not washed my hands in his blood, my blood. In her most silent moments, she called out to her father.

She expected no response. But, maybe! Consolation seems so far away otherwise, she thought. Somehow, we've all been miss-educated. Somehow, we all seem to have unlearned the "Golden Rule", and everyone's personal safety is always in jeopardy. I think that at school we must consider offering a course in human fragility.

Even as other social organizations try to deal with these issues, Louise thought, high schools must join in the fray. No! I don't want to instill fear in them, but our kids need to know that everything that we are is so easily broken. Mind, body, spirit! They need to know that few people who are born into this world live through it all without acquiring holes in their lives. Even high school students need to know that none of us are invulnerable, that their own youthful glow is only a temporary thing. They need to know long before hand about the rights and the wrongs of living and how easily we are ended.

On this sunlit afternoon, she sat in her kitchen. All the familiar things, the things she'd accumulated over the years surrounded her. Christine was visiting with Mabel, "catching up" as her girl was fond of saying. Wallace would be home next week, and she had already begun her lesson preps for the upcoming semester. None of this, however, brought sufficient relief to what she now called her troubled spirit.

Her brother's death had created an empty space in her soul that Louise doubted she'd ever be able to fill. Each day, she followed the news media as she had always done. She needed a sign, something that would tell her that justice would ultimately be served, that somehow some semblance of fairness would ultimately prevail. She spent hours watching the news shows on cable television. She began to seek out other things to do. Nothing new appeared. It was always the same. On the television, loaded words and empty rhetoric did exactly what was expected. Each day, she questioned some of the language she heard and which was being pushed out onto the public.

On those occasions when she heard words like "radicalization" liberally tossed about with only the purpose of creating fear, she laughed.

It is usually those people who scream the loudest about radicalization, she thought, who are responsible for its birth. Will they never understand that being discriminatory, offensive, and insensitive towards people always brings negative results? Mired in their own fears, it is those who are afraid of losing their imagined power over others who are the first to do murder because of those fears. In the end, she pleaded of herself, it must be these people who are held accountable.

Fear is the ultimate means of control, she thought. With little or no awareness of the facts, the fearful are often controlled more by their own fears than seems logically reasonable.

Students of history, she thought, seem to have learned how it is that autocratic politicians use fear to gain power over large numbers of people. For them, it is a tool that is as old as recorded time. In many places on this earth, even law enforcement employs this tool. No one questions it. Perhaps some members of law enforcement must also learn that when people are wavering on the precipice between life and death, a tiny spark can ignite a revolution. History has repeated itself far more frequently than any of us is willing to acknowledge.

Not too long ago, fear drove mobs of angry and hateful people to annihilate whole communities right here in North America, and utterly ended the lives of those who were not like themselves. I am sure, she thought, that only a few teachers will speak of a history that is riddled with this kind of behavior, of periods of time when fear, alone, drove people into war with their neighbors.

Yes, I have Wallace and Christine. I am not alone, but I am still fearful. There seems to be very little I can be sure of. I believe that I will be okay. Won't I? When her thoughts moved to the new reality of her own life she did, however, feel a small twinge of disconnection. There was a truth she had yet to acknowledge. A mother I never knew, she mourned, a father who is also gone now. Even the last of her blood links, the one that she had taken for granted, George, was no longer there. However, her husband and her daughter continued to provide her more incentive to keep moving forward. She also had to acknowledge that diving from the cliffs of her imagination into her innermost and often negative thoughts had also provided little relief.

In the end, she thought, maybe it is true that the most powerful thing is love. How else can it be? I am still here, and my deceased dear ones will live on in my memory. I will love them all forever. Even my unknown mother!

Louise felt her entire body jerk as if grabbed by an invisible hand. A single jerk! That was all! And she remembered that she had been home for several weeks, mourning, commiserating, blaming, wallowing in anger, and trying very hard to forget that all that is born into this world transforms, dies. She also remembered that the one person she needed to talk with was nearby and all she had to do was to call. She knew that the call would have to be done. She knew also that something else was brewing inside of her.

She had attempted to assign some reason behind the events of the past two months. Suddenly, the journey she had embarked upon shortly after Henry's death came into focus. Everything happens for a reason, she thought. Was I supposed to see all that human misery, even the death of someone I loved? She shuddered at the thought of all the spiritual confusion she was experiencing. Recalling the dream in which she and her father had met and talked, she could almost hear his voice as he spoke with brief clarity. She remembered precisely what he had said to her.

"First," he had said, "heal yourself. Then heal those around you."

Louise felt the call of the sweat lodge. She felt the heat rise from the Grandmothers. Rising from her seat at the table, she walked over to the wall phone. Feeling much lighter, she dialed the telephone number to Sohi's Lodge.

"Louise," Sohi answered, "I have been waiting for your call."

Once they were passed the initial greetings, Louise immediately concluded that she didn't have much time to waste.

"I need to see you," she said. "Much has happened."

"I know," Sohi said. "Are you okay?"

"I'm getting better. . . . I think it is time, though, for me to explore my own spiritual connections."

"I will be in town tomorrow," Sohi said. "If you like, I can drop by and we can talk about your goal and how we can get you there."

"Perfect," Louise responded. "Until tomorrow! Oh, by the way, how is everybody there? Is Snow Owl still there?"

24

"It was the dream," Louise said, looking into Sohi's eyes. "As the real world was exploding and everything was happening around me, I felt trapped inside the very dream in which I'd already seen most of what was happening, and I couldn't get out. Throughout the whole dream, and on those separate occasions when it occurred, there was never any indication that George would be involved or be the second victim. Now, I know just one thing. As much as I regret losing my brother, I also regret witnessing the death of that child."

"That's very powerful," Sohi replied. "You know, it takes a special gift to know what is happening to you when it is happening like that. That gives us a good idea about where you are right now. . . . avHHHhkkkkll Have you thought about what you want to do?"

Louise paused as she recalled the time when she first met the woman with whom she sat and talked. It was at the Home where her father had lived and died. They became fast friends. Since then, all the time she had spent at the Lodge where Sohi lived was now written indelibly on her soul.

She remembered those wondrous times in the sweat lodge with the grandmothers, when supernaturally hot powers ripped away the aches and pains of her life and altered her perceptions on just about everything. All of this was now ingrained into everything that she was and had become. She now believed that what happened during those days had possibly even saved her life. And it was Sohi who had helped her along the way.

"If I could just find the words to relay to you something my father said to me in another dream just before he passed," Louise said, "maybe you can help me to better understand what is really happening to me. He seemed certain that somewhere in me there is the ability to heal. Not just for myself, but other people too.

"To tell you the truth, the time we spent in Philadelphia revealed many personal discoveries to me, discoveries about me. I thought about how for the longest time, I've been so content with my life that I had forgotten that there's a terrible amount of suffering going on in this world, and it doesn't seem to know anything about race and gender. I know it sounds idealistic, but sometimes I wish I could find a way to bring a lasting spiritual health to all of the people who need it. If it is in me, I need to find that place that my father spoke of, and I need to plea for the power to use it."

"Then, we'll also need to find the time when you are free to pursue your own vision quest," Sohi nodded. "As a seeker, you will be received. We will complete the purification process in the sweat lodge. Then, when it is time, you will go on your quest. If is meant to be, you will receive the power. Before that, though, there are some medicine people I want to introduce you to. Just let me know what your schedule is like after school begins. We'll go from there. . . . There's no hurry, Louise. Breathe deeply. It will all work out, my sister."

"I'm still a few years away from retirement," Louise responded. She heard the uncertainty in her own voice.

"We must act sooner than that," Sohi said. "You have much to do, and we will find a way."

Louise nodded. Suddenly, all her fears subsided. She felt like a child anxious to play with some of the other playground toys. Didn't I read somewhere, she asked silently, that that is what consciousness is. A playground!

"Thank you, my friend," Louise said to Sohi. "I know that one of the things you and I talked about before we went to Philadelphia was what could possibly happen there. Well, something did happen, and since I got home, I have dwelled in a world of negativity. I know now that it is because we talked about this potential, and I am left completely exhausted and uncertain. You see, I believe that I am inflicting further wounds onto myself with all this fear. The very memory of that night, of my brother sprawled on the ground, of my own hands traveling over his dead body will be a part of me until I die."

"You're right," Sohi said. "It is a terrible thing to have to be there and watch your loved ones die. Especially under those circumstances! The people I will introduce you to will help you with this. They have gone through what you have, in their own ways.

"You once asked if it was necessary for you to witness so much human misery. I have read that there are spiritual teachers who believe that sometimes it is necessary for the student to see the whole picture, to see that all of human suffering and human joy is included in that one picture."

"Of course," Louise smiled. "I'm not completely sure, but I think I can understand the balance. I imagine that throughout the world, so many people have attempted to find that balance. Daddy used to tell me how it was when he was young. He had but one dream, and that was to become a Tibetan lama. He thought they were the most balanced people on the earth. From what I know of them, they are certainly a special people."

"Yes," Sohi nodded. "Many people wander through the desert, in the biblical sense, and sometimes it truly does feel as if you have become a spiritual fountain of youth, especially for those who are true. They are renewed. That is what I am told."

25

Then it was September. Joining with her colleagues, Louise smiled more frequently as the doors to the school were opened and classes were resumed. Quickly finding that by absorbing herself into her work, she was able to put the past disastrous summer into a much clearer perspective. By familiarizing herself with the new students in her classes, she distanced herself even further from the unpleasant memories, and she had managed to push them into the background. Slowly, the summer began to fade, and she was suddenly able to focus on her 'quest'.

Though she saw no immediate exit for taking time off from work, the very thought of her vision quest was now a part of her daily routine. She realized that the thought itself had become a revelation. She had never believed that she could want something so intensely. Her new schedule, however, was filled with an entirely new set of activities, and she was left with no choice except to delay her plans.

When she spoke with Sohi, they mutually agreed that the school year could be strenuous, and that they may have to wait until the end of May of next year. They also agreed to the arrangement for her to attend the sweat lodge once a month in preparation for her 'quest'.

On her trip to the Lodge in late October, after spending some time with the Grandmothers in the sweat lodge, she and Sohi went for a long walk into the forest. The sky was overcast with thick clouds, and they were surrounded by thickets of trees that were still ablaze with the colors of autumn. A steady breeze swept over them as they moved deeper into the forest. During much of their hike, they were quiet. Then, when they were more than a mile from the Lodge, Sohi spoke.

"I wanted to show you this place," Sohi said. "When it is time, your place will be in this forest. There are many places where you can set up your tent. You choose. Some people like to go to the top of that hill over there. You know that you will be alone for a few days, but don't worry. There are no dangerous animals here."

"It is almost impossible to believe," Louise responded, "that I am here, and that I am preparing to do something I should have done a long time ago."

"It was not your time before now," Sohi said. "We must go back now."

By the time they arrived back at the Lodge, Louise felt exhilarated. Her anticipation of the upcoming 'quest' had increased exponentially, but she accepted that she still had to wait for another seven months. She would finish the school year while continuing her preparation in the sweat lodge, and she would return to this very place to experience what could well be a part of her destiny.

The mixture of high school football and the traditional holidays like Christmas and New Year arrived without any unusual fanfare. Christine, Louise, and Wallace celebrated with Wallace's mother. Then the holidays were over, and Louise was suddenly back in her classroom to watch as her students returned. Each of them was well rested and aglow from the time they had been off and the gifts they had received. They even expressed enthusiasm about the remainder of the school year.

When the graduation ceremonies occurred at the beginning of May, Louise was once again all smiles as students she known for years were suddenly embarking on new adventures. Some were going to college. Others were joining the military. Some were even getting married. While she greeted each of them with good wishes and hopes for the future, the events of last summer lingered in her heart and began to resurge into her thoughts.

From that point, the days moved quickly. Suddenly, it was the end of May. While she had been so caught up with events at the school, she remembered that she had had a whole year to prepare, to shore up her own belief system, and she was ready. Last year, when Sohi escorted her to the spot where should she would remain for four days and four nights when she was ready, she finally concluded that the time has arrived. I am here, she thought.

With Wallace driving the car, the trip was very different. He had insisted that he would accompany her to the Lodge. She didn't argue. She was quietly pleased that he had adopted a serious stance in what she was about to do. After arriving, they paused briefly at the big Lodge house where Wallace parked the car and pulled the little tent from the trunk. Then they walked through the forest to the spot that Sohi had shown her.

The small knoll seemed to magnetize her. Surrounded by a grove of poplars and a few straggling jack pines, the hill was high enough that its top reached the overhead canopy. She and Sohi had gathered the cedar branches she would need in a different location.

She had never imagined it would be like this, she thought as she looked around. The place was seething with life. Chirping, brightly colored birds flew everywhere. Looking around, she decided just to see what she could see. In May, she thought, this forest is a wonderland.

Looking at Wallace, she nodded toward the knoll, and they began the ascent up the narrow, steep path that led to the top of the hill. On reaching the top, they were both pleasantly surprised to discover that the top was flat and smooth, roughly thirty feet in diameter, and had clearly been used before.

They mounted the tent in exactly the middle of the thirty-foot diameter. Buried deep in the forest, Louise knew that the spot was isolated and safe. She also knew that they were about a mile and a half away from Sohi's Lodge.

"Will you be alright here?" Wallace finally asked.

"I do believe that I will" she replied.

"You know, you can always change your mind."

"No chance of that," she said. "This is something I've wanted for a very long time."

When the job of setting up the tent was completed, Wallace and she talked further.

"Chrissy and I will be here for the feast," he said. "Do what you've got to do."

Finally, he hugged her tightly and left her to return to the city, and to look after Christine during these days when her mother would not be at home.

She could not recall a time when she was so alone, when nothing familiar existed around her. This, she thought, is where I learn what real freedom is. For four days and four nights she would be unencumbered. She would be alone with only the trees and the wind and the spirits and her own thoughts. As she threw the cedar ring of protection around the tent, her excitement began to rise. After checking the four colored flags, which were the gateways to the north and the east and the west and the south, she inhaled deeply and smiled as she sat down on the ground at the door of the little tent.

From her high vantage point, Louise saw the green leafy canopy directly in front of her and stretching endlessly into the horizon. She smelled the receding freshness of late spring. She watched as birds ascended through the tree tops and flit off into the evening sky. Probably in search of food, she thought. Food! She would not eat or drink during this time, and right now she felt only indifference about that. She was not hungry. She did not expect that she would be hungry.

She had made it. Sometimes, she thought, the goals we set remain so far away. It feels like they will never happen. Sitting in front of her little tent, she felt the approach of the night. With only the sounds of the birds to keep her company, she knew with absolute certainty that she was embarked on not only her vision quest but a more fulfilling life as well. She prayed that she would receive the blessings she sought.

From far away, Louise heard the drum beat lift its voice into the darkening sky. She saw the Evening Star. The air around her was distinctly cooler, and the growing darkness was beginning to make her eyelids heavy. The activities of the day had moved very fast and she was tired. She retreated into the tent.

Though it was a small and tight space, she still wore her plaid wool jacket and a pair of heavy underwear, she was warm and comfortable. She could not anticipate anything about the immediate future, about what was going to happen. Even tonight, she thought. She felt no fear.

Sitting comfortably with her legs bent at the knees and her ankles folded one across the other, she meditated. Outside the tent, complete darkness descended, and the jack pines began to sing with the rising wind.

As the evening wore on and with no external stimuli, Louise soon lost consciousness of time. She knew only that it was night. Though she was tired, she could not sleep. Her energy levels were too high. Her eyes were closed, yet her senses relating to the external world were on alert. Her awareness was suddenly all encompassing, and she knew the place where she was as if she had been there an entire lifetime.

Then, she heard their approach. At first, they were far away. Over and over, what sounded like giants stomping across the world toward the tent seemed to shake the very earth on which she sat. When the booming sound joined with the howling wind and swept the little tent to and fro, she spread her arms and touched both walls of the little tent. Louise was especially startled when a series of mighty thrusts from some great and invisible hand pushed the top of the tent downward again and again.

In the chaos of the moment, Louise almost succumbed. She almost screamed, but her wits were heightened. With no idea about where this newfound courage came from, she knew only that this was neither the place nor the time to cringe away into the darkness. She had come here for them. To honor them! To seek their assistance! She was unafraid, and she remained quiet. Long before they left her, and with her legs still folded underneath her, Louise fell asleep.

"Well, my daughter!" Henry said. "Look at where you are. I am so proud of you."

"I have lost George," she cried. "It is only me now."

"Yes. . . . George is here," Henry responded, "with me and your mother! Because he came to us so suddenly, he had a hard time adjusting. But he's good now. And no! You are not alone. There is an army of good-willed people who support you."

"Do you know why I am doing this?" She asked.

"Of course!" Henry laughed. "Don't you know? Look back over the patterns of your life, even from your child-hood. You are here because you will never be able to deny who and what you are. And it appears you are destined to do some good. . . ."

Though she slept, she was acutely aware of the unending cycle that turned night into day. She did not recall the number of days that had passed, days during which she sat in the little tent, but she knew when day became night, and she felt the wheel of life turn. For what seemed like eternity, Louise drifted from dream to dream.

At first, she was astonished by the presence of people who had been in and out of her life over the years. With a life-altering surprise, she was suddenly the unborn fetus, snug and safe inside her mother's womb. She remained there for as long as she could, listening to the beating heart of the woman who would bring her into the world. When she left that place, her consciousness was far greater than she had ever known. She was aware of the instant dissolution of her angst regarding her mother. Ensuing immediately behind her sudden spiritual liberation, Louise knew that she was blessed, and she was able to envision the past, the present, and the future. She even visited briefly with her deceased family, and they greeted her with loving eyes and smiles.

Then, still moving, she descended into the hot melting center of the earth only to rise to the summit of the mountaintop. For the very first time in her life, she began to understand the spiritual significance of her own existence in the universe.

Suddenly, all of time was irrelevant, and space was the entire universe wrapped in brilliant light and emptiness. Then something swung past her. Vast in size and pulsating like heartbeats, huge orbs vibrated around her and signaled that life and death was the natural flow of existence, and that it was often far swifter than the blinking eye. She watched as distant stars glittered cold light, sputtered, and blinked out.

As a gust of wind, she flew through a dozen ancient villages located in the high mountains of Africa and Asia. She touched the masked men and women, steeped in ritual as they greeted her, welcomed her. She joined her own voice with those of the monks in the high Himalayas. It was as if they all had been waiting for her, and they welcomed her. She saw them all. She heard them all. She flew through them all and melted into them until she became them, and she was the air and the earth itself.

"Time to go home," the voice called.

She heard the voice. It was faraway, but it was strong. She felt the sound of the voice begin to pull her back into this world. Though she could not immediately identify who it was, Louise groggily unzipped and folded back the tent door. Her eyes screamed painfully as the bright sunlight streamed into the tiny tent. Sohi stood just outside the cedar circle. She was grinning.

"Is it really time?" Louise asked. "Have I been here that long?"

Sohi nodded. "Yes, my sister. This is the morning of your fifth day. This phase is over. How do you feel?"

Louise crawled out of the tent and tried to stand, only to find that her legs were stiff and screaming from having sat for so long. It was only when she stepped gingerly toward the ring of cedar that she felt the circulation painfully return to her legs.

"The world feels brighter," Louise grinned. "I have never seen colors so vivid."

"It is you who shines!" Sohi retorted, adding to Louise's joy. "Still, after four days and four nights, we must get you cleaned up. The feast is ready and the people are waiting!"

"I have to dismantle the tent," Louise hesitated.

"No, it'll be brought to the Lodge."

As they descended the path and began the walk back to the Lodge, Louise paused and looked back at the knoll. Through the trees, she could even see the little tent on top of the hill. She knew deep in her soul that the spot would forever represent a sacred place for her, a place where she had undergone a transformation so complete that the closest thing to it was when she gave birth to Christine. That little tent on top of the hill is where it all occurred, she thought. And she would take this knowledge to her grave. Soon, another seeker will sit on the hilltop.

"On this day," Sohi's smile was exultant, "you are a holy woman. Remember to pay close attention to your dreams. The elders are waiting for you. We will eat, and you will receive your name."

26

Tom Yates' retirement party was in full bloom by the time Louise and Wallace who had walked the few short blocks from their house and arrived at the house in River Heights. Happily, the evening sun served to remind everyone that it was still a warm day. Both outside and inside the cute little gray bungalow, a mass of people, mostly former students and other academics who had worked with Yates, were gathered into small groups. Many people stood laughing and talking and sipping glasses of wine while listening to pop music playing on the radio. For some, the party was also a renewal and a continuation of old friendships. When Tom Yates saw Wallace and Louise come through the door, he rushed over to greet them both.

"I'm really glad you guys made it," he grinned.

"We are too!" Louise laughed. "Is this really a retirement party? You have left a huge impression on a lot people. I didn't know you were so popular. Where's Barbara?"

"Ah, she's around here somewhere. As to my popularity, my dear, the booze is free," Yates responded with a comical expression of gloom on his face and a shrug of his shoulders. "That'll bring 'em every time."

"Incidentally," Louise said, "I wanted to congratulate you on your success with the Human Project."

"Thank you, but it was really your partner and people like him who made it all happen. I am indebted to all of them. In some cases, however, we lost a lot more than we should have. Would you please accept my belated condolences for your brother?"

"Thank you," she replied. "By now everybody knows what's happening down there. Men, particularly young men, are at risk. My brother was just one of many. I hope that doesn't sound too harsh."

"As you say, we all know what's happening. I can only pray that this phase will not last forever. Meanwhile, I hope the three of us will have some time to talk before the evening is over," Yates said. "I have something to tell you, Louise."

"Then, we'll talk," Louise smiled. Having no idea what they would talk about, she could only wait to find out. After all, she had waited more than a year for this conversation with Tom Yates. Wallace had warned her long ago that Yates might request her participation with The Human Project.

"By the way," Yates called as he began to walk away, "I hear you have undergone some cross-cultural transformations of your own lately. A vision quest, was it? I'd certainly like to hear more about that!"

Turning to Wallace, Louise looked into his eyes with accusatory questions. "Did you do this?"

"No," Wallace laughed. "But this is it, Kiddo. Don't say you weren't warned. He may be retiring, but he is not going to just fade into the woodwork. Even after he is gone, he will still be here. He is an honored member of our faculty. I guess I should be happy, too. I get to take over his job and his office at the end of the month."

"What? You're going to be the new dean?" Louise' eyes were wide with surprise.

"You got it, Sweetheart!" Wallace grinned. "Your old man is now the new Dean of the Anthropology department."

"And you kept all of this to yourself," Louise struggled to control her rising anger.

"I didn't want to be premature," Wallace replied. "What would have been the point of getting your hopes up? My own were already too high, and I just got confirmation yesterday."

"This is excellent news, Wally!" Louise said. "I suppose this means you'll be home a lot more. Doesn't it?"

"That may be more convenient than you know," Wallace smiled.

"Why? What do you mean?" Louise quizzed.

"We'll talk about this more after you have spoken with Tom. Listen, Baby, mingle. I am sure there are people here you know. I see Ortega Ruiz has come up from the states for this event. I must speak with him. Okay?"

"Okay," she nodded. "But I will find out what's going on! I always do, you know!"

Moving away from the front door where Tom had met them, she slowly looked around the room. Finally, she spotted other people that she knew. Grabbing a glass of wine from the table, Louise weaved her way through the crowded room toward the sliding back door. Barbara

Yates sat on the patio with two other women, all of whom were laughing.

"Louise!" Barbara shouted. "How long has it been? You look great! Come, sit down here. You haven't met my sister Blanche. . . . Blanche has never been happy with the fact that between us, I am the oldest. . . . And this lady is my dear friend Snalda McDonald. Doctor Snalda McDonald! As you may already have gathered, everybody here is and was involved with the Human Project in one way or another. It is wonderful to meet so many people."

Smiling, Louise stepped onto the patio and joined with the three women. Sitting down on one of the few remaining unoccupied chairs, she was suddenly conscious that she was looking at the three women with eyes that saw the world differently than it had only a few years ago. She had been reborn, and she had become increasingly aware that no matter where she was, for now she carried the little tent on the hill foremost in her consciousness.

"Louise," Snalda McDonald said, "is it true that you were born in Philadelphia? Are you still an American citizen?"

Louise nodded. "Yes," she said, "to both of your questions. Because I couldn't give it up, I became a dual citizen years ago. Like my father, I believe that, no matter what, the land out of which we are born is a part of our very souls. Besides, we all know that Philadelphia is a special place. The birthplace of the nation and all that."

Snalda McDonald seemed both surprised and pleased with Louise's response. McDonald was a short, stout woman who rarely deviated from the style of clothing she wore: a white blouse, covered by a gray vest and a gray skirt. She had been a nun for many years, but she had also been intellectually restless. After obtaining her doctorate in Sociology, she remained embedded in her faith and refused to leave the convent where she also taught classes. The woman's hair was cropped and peppery gray, and her blue eyes sat deep in a face that reflected a serious and active involvement with whatever she did.

"You guys were so busy during the time that we were there." Louise offered. "A lot was happening. My sister-in-law and I attended one of the interviews that Wallace filmed. It was an amazing thing to behold. It is always surprising to me how easy we forget about the pain that other people suffer."

"Yes." McDonald said slowly. "Some of us, however, can't forget. We are confronted by it every day. You can feel its noxious breath as it screams into your face, always leaving a residue of fear and hopelessness. I think that is why we are still at it. Other people in other parts of these two countries are doing similar things. Many are traveling about the countries and creating documentaries with enormous scopes.

"It is imperative that we record the present state of social injustice in both Canada and the U.S. The truth about poverty must be exposed, because it is everywhere. For me, after everything else, it is exciting to be involved with all this. Of course, the change we are all hoping for will not happen overnight. It never does, and we all know it. There are times when we are consoled. On those occasions, we learn that many of the people who are still living under those dire circumstances also learn that they are not alone. As small as it is, it gives us all a hope we did not have before. Even the Sisters at the Home where I live express gushing enthusiasm. I have only one concern, however.

"It's just that people are often reserved and fearful," McDonald continued. "That's when we learn that many people dislike telling the truth about what is really happening in their lives. I have seen that unless they are in formal Confession, too many people resort to running away. Seeing a nonexistent danger, many people prefer to hide away behind whatever walls they can construct as if they have no responsibility even for their own lives. It makes our jobs doubly hard. We strive to rectify that, and we will keep striving."

"The Project is very young," Barbara inserted. The setting sun glistened on Barbara's dark hair. "If I am right, it will grow and it will spread to other parts of the world where poverty and hopelessness hold death grips on so many people. . . . Louise, what are your plans now since your partner has become the new dean?"

"Support him as best I can!" Louise smiled. "I just found out about it a few minutes ago. I am very pleased for him. As for me. I do have other things going on, however. I'm still teaching. I have also begun working with First Nations people in ways I could never have imagined. And I have a daughter who is undergoing physiological changes and who is not very far from being a teenager. I love this busy life though! It's rather like an expansion of consciousness, you know."

Again, Snalda McDonald smiled her approval. "You have a clean and wonderful energy, Louise. Did you know that?"

"Thank you," Louise grinned. As she spoke, she also envisioned the little tent in which she had sat for 4 days and nights. "I really didn't think about it. But, you know, a girl can hope."

All four women burst into laughter. Though the women reveled in their newfound comradeship, none of them failed to notice the three men who came through the back door onto the patio to join them. Each of the men carried a folding seat with him.

"Ladies," Barbara exclaimed, "we are caught!"

"Come on, now," Tom Yates laughed. "Tell the truth. You don't mind, do you? Anyway, I thought that, if it is at all possible, we would have a bit of a gab fest out here."

Louise was suddenly aware of her own self-consciousness She couldn't be sure but looking around she noticed that for a single moment, all the other eyes on the patio were locked on her, she looked at Wallace who had just arrived with Tom Yates and Ortega Ruiz.

"Louise," Tom Yates spoke without hesitation, "I am most anxious to hear about your vision quest. What a surprise! I believe that there are not a lot people brave enough to venture into that kind of cross-cultural world anymore. The very idea of spending days by oneself and not indulging our appetites is frightful. It is a spiritual adventure. I understand that. What made you decide to do it?"

"At first, I think it was curiosity," she responded. "My father had done it years ago, and he was a different man from the one I'd known as child. I wanted to find out what he did. Then, quite unexpectedly, I needed to do it for me. As it happens, I believe the one thing I can say is that it is a very primal experience. A form of regression seems to occur, even to the point of pre-birth. Long-held anxieties and fears are finally resolved. When it was over, I walked into a new world."

"Remarkable!" Yates laughed. "I have had occasion to look at some of the mythology that surrounds this practice. It is very old. Good on you! Now, that said, I would like to talk with you about a challenge I recently received.

"With the help of present company, I will try to explain what this challenge consists of."

Louise felt her curiosity begin to rise. The glass of wine she had drunk relaxed her, and she was more than willing to engage in this long- awaited conversation.

"The Human Project," Tom Yates began, "has far exceeded our expectations. We did not set out to become politicians or even politically involved, and I insist we maintain that stance. Political forces far beyond ourselves, however, have been watching us.

"Not long ago, we were approached by a representative from the UN. It appears that that august organization is continuously looking for imaginative ways to deal with the tremendous diversity of the human population and experience on this earth. Tell me, Louise. What does diversity mean to you?"

The question came out of nowhere. She knew that somewhere she had an answer, and she also knew that the answer she would provide was not the one she would have provided a year ago.

"Remember that I am only a high school English teacher. I could easily offer the dictionary definition which is little more than a statement about human differences, but I believe that diversity is more than that. I believe it is the essence of humanity," Louise said. "Any ideology that stands in opposition to diversity does so with a fair amount of disingenuousness. Even the natural order of things is built on variation and diversity. I would never say that it's wrong for people to believe in themselves, but when those beliefs become tribal and excludes all who do not look alike or think alike or behave alike, we all have a problem.

She could feel her words rise from her abdomen. "Ours is one of the most unique species on the earth. Aside from our ability to reason, nowhere on earth are there two human beings who are completely identical. Even twins! Look closely and you will find their differences, their individual uniqueness. I imagine that this singularity applies to nearly eight billion human souls on this earth. We all look differently. We speak different languages. We live out our lives under different belief systems. And, yes, we also believe differently even about God.

"I believe that to gain a fuller understanding of diversity," Louise continued, "we need only to look at our innermost selves to discover our own unique and individual differences. It has been my experience, however, that most of us are far more susceptible to the external influences around us than we are to the truth of the inner worlds.

Those inner worlds I mentioned are where I believe diversity really lives for each of us."

"Then, with a bit of prodding," Snalda McDonald responded, "most people – at least those who want to – can come to understand that diversity is also about universal unification?"

"Now that you've said that, I agree with you more than you know," Laughing, Louise nodded. "And everybody knows that the topic isn't very difficult for us teachers. We simply use a bit of persuasive advertising."

"Well said," Tom Yates laughed.

Looking at Wallace, Louise sensed even more questions rising into her thoughts. Am I in an interview, she asked silently. What is going on?

"Louise," Tom Yates said, "I would like to invite you to join with us. But, more than that, I believe your superb response to my 'diversity' question is beyond what I think many people understand. I, however, understand it! Next, and this is the one I have mulled over for a while: I wish to get your permission to submit your name to my friend, the representative from the UN I was telling you about. It seems that they are seeking people who can fill some vacancies in their Cultural and Goodwill Ambassadors departments.

"The reason I ask you about this is because I believe that someone with your qualifications, someone who has the kind of experience you have along with mental flexibility, would do exceedingly well. Now, if you need some time to think about all of this, take as much as you need.

But not too much! We would like to respond to them as soon as possible."

"I am honored," Louise said haltingly, "that you thought of me. Because of what I have been doing, this is a truly appealing opportunity. With my hubby's help, I'll let you know very soon."

Around them, evening became dusk as the night approached. Their conversations continued as other people began to drift onto the patio to say goodbye. Louise also felt that it was time to go home. Christine, she thought, was probably at home now, waiting for them. After offering their salutations, they began the short walk along a few blocks to their own house.

27

"That was exciting," she said as they walked along the sidewalk. They were still a block away from their own house, "What will Tom and Barbara do now?"

"Oh, he'll be around," Wallace replied. "They both will. There is some talk about a trip to Europe. Nothing is firm, however."

"Wally," Louise said, "Let's talk about something else. There are some things I'd like to discuss with you. It's taken me forever, but I think the vision quest has helped me to finally bring a summation to the past. You see, the thing that was predominate in all of this was my own feelings about my mother. As you know, she was an activist and she was driven by the vicious murders of those children in Alabama. For a while, Daddy felt that he was completely alone, because Mama was devoted to the cause, so much so that she imperiled her own life.

"I grew up with a lot of anger churning in my belly, and it was about her. When I needed her to be there, she was not. I figured that she had abandoned George and me because she did not love us. She didn't abandon us, of course. She simply wanted a safer world for us, and that desire got her killed. I can relate to this mostly because

I find myself saying the same thing about our own child. Hopefully, I will survive where my mother could not.

"Now, I can clearly see what happened to Daddy, what drove him away from his family and his country. Grammie used to tell me that if he had not left, he would have been like so many other black men and women. He would be either dead or in prison.

"She told me when that church was bombed in Alabama and those children were murdered, Daddy felt that, like so many other black military men, he had been betrayed by his own homeland. He had served in the military overseas and he had fought for his country. The deaths of those children told him that no matter what he did, it meant nothing.

"Then, when he finally came home, he repeatedly suffered assaults on both his person and his dignity by law enforcement. Those were the days when Jim Crow and racial profiling was in full bloom. When my mother was killed by that police officer, Daddy went a bit crazy. Grandma Cora stopped him before he could do something bad, something that would have torn all of us apart forever.

"I know that you understand that I'm recalling all of this in an effort to make a decision, don't you?"

"I know," Wallace said. "I think you have already made a decision. All you got to do now is let me know what it is."

"You're right! I just had to be clear about my own feelings."

"You're going to do it, aren't you?"

"Yes," she replied. "It is very likely that I am going to do this. It means an early retirement from the school, but I think it is time for me do something else. I do remember when we were in Philadelphia and Revered Latimore telling me that I am very much like my mother. Who knew? Also, when we were in Philadelphia, I would have given anything to have been able to do something. Especially on that night when George was killed. Now that chance is here. I just might be able to help a lot of people. Especially Sohi and her community. I love them, and I also think our daughter would be especially proud to see her mother as an ambassador."

"As will her mother's partner," Wallace laughed. "I'm with you all the way. You go for it!"

Printed in Canada